THE CASEBOOK OF THE SPIRIT-SEEKER

Cover Art illustrated by Mary Landro.
Socials: @mlandart
Website: mlandart.com

Published by Dark Titan Publishing.
A subsidiary of Dark Titan Imaginations and Products.
A division of The Dark Titan Company.

Paperback ISBN: 979-8-9875065-6-1
eBook ISBN: 979-8-9875065-7-8

darktitanpublishing.com

TY'RON W. C. ROBINSON II

CONTENTS

THE TALE OF THE HAUNTING

Occult Detective Travis Vail set out on his investigation to a mansion which is documented to be a very haunted location. Wearing his black coat with slacks, Vail arrives in the city of Hartford, Connecticut, where the mansion is located on the outskirts of the city. Vail gets to the mansion, known as the Rosebane Mansion. Outside of the mansion is its current owner, Lloyd Sharp. Sharp extends his hand as a greeting to Vail.

"Welcome to Rosebane Mansion, Mr. Vail." Sharp said. Vail shook his hand in greeting and allowed Sharp to invite him inside the mansion.

Within the mansion's interior is a beautiful structure for a century-year-old building. The walls are made of granite marble with historical paintings and picture frames across. The flooring was made of hardwood. Vail quickly examines the mansion's interior.

"What happened here that caused the haunting?" Vail said.

"The former residents were unaware of what was buried here centuries ago." Sharp said. "One day, their son was digging in the backyard and discovered a skeleton with Indian artifacts."

"An Indian burial ground, you say.' Vail said.

"Of course." Sharp said. "Once the parents discovered it, they had it taken away, which later became a regret to them as the poltergeist activities began to occur."

"Truly a mistake they made.' Vail said. "So, I've been brought here to investigate these haunting?"

Sharp brought Vail into the bedroom section of the mansion upper floors. Inside were a total of six rooms, the master bedroom belonged to the parents, another to their son, and four for guests. Vail walked through every bedroom, scavenging the entire location for anything resourceful. Sharp watched him as he went through every room like a focused individual. After Vail completed his search through the rooms. Walking through a corridor, Sharp took Vail out to the backyard. Once outside, Sharp pointed to the now buried sport of where the Indian burial was originally located. Vail walked over to the spot and rubbed the dirt on the ground. He raised his head, looking around the backyard. He turned to Sharp and thanked him for showing him the areas of the mansion,

"I take it you're ready to do your work.' Sharp said.

"Yes I am." Vail said.

Vail went to the nearest museum and did research on the mansion and the land. his hotel room and began setting up his equipment. From holy water to crosses to a book that is encrypted with proper ways to end curses or send spirits back into their world. After he left the room. He went back to the mansion to begin his investigation upon its encounters.

Later that night, Vail returned to the mansion, alone. He found the key to the front door underneath the movable block by the door. He entered the mansion and shut the door. No lights were on throughout the mansion, only the moonlight. Vail walked around the mansion, pulling out a book that contained previous reports and encounters inside the mansion.

"Very well." He said. "You have me here all alone. So, I would demand that you reveal yourself to me or at least give me a sign of your presence to start with."

The mansion is silent to the point where if a pen would fall onto the wooden floor, it would make a louder sound. Vail slowly walked through the corridor of the mansion, surrounded by frames of the previous owners of the mansion and the land of which it lies upon. He looked at the frames and walked over to one that resembled a English settler. Once he stopped to look, a banging sound was heard down the corridor. Vail paused.

"I see you're trying to get my attention."

He walked down to the end of the corridor. Once at the end, he sees nothing in sight. He heard another banging sound that came from the bedroom areas.

"I want to speak with the spirit of the burial ground." He said. "I know you're here inside this mansion with me."

Vail continued down the corridor as one of the picture frames instantly flew off the wall and down the other end of the corridor. Vail looked and ran after it. He reached the other end of the corridor and the frame was nowhere in sight. He turned back around walking upstairs toward the bedrooms. He heard a distant moan near the rooms.

"You're getting better at this."

The lamp on the side of the bed levitated and slammed itself against the wall. Vail walked into the bedroom, which was a guest room.

"Very violent I noticed."

"*Get Out.*"

The words caught Vail's attention as he heard the distinctive voice coming from the master bedroom nearby. He walked into the room and it was quiet, everything is the same as it was earlier in the day. Vail reached into his coat pocket and pulled out a cleansing artifact that he received during his research into Indian burial grounds.

"I suggest you prepare to see the other side."

Vail began blessing the entire mansion with the cleansing. As he walked through the mansion saying the blessing, more sounds of banging occurred along with moans and distant yelling. Vail ignored the sounds and decided to head into the backyard.

As Vail walked outside in the backyard, he noticed the wind beginning to blow. He continued the cleansing as he walked near the burial ground. Vail paused for a second as he seen what appeared to be fire coming from the burial ground. Vail kneeled in front of the burial and held the cleansing over it, blessing it once more. As he spoke louder while blessing, he looked up and seen an apparition of what appeared to be a Indian man, wearing Native American wardrobe. The Indian apparition stared at Vail, who did the same.

"I see you as you can see me." Vail said to the apparition. "It's time you leave this place and enter the afterlife."

The wind slowly calmed, and the fire vanished along with the apparition. Vail walked back into the mansion and he felt a sense of calmness. Vail walked through the mansion for a final time to double check. Every room he went into he felt a sense of calmness and peace.

Later in the morning, Sharp returned to the mansion as Vail began to leave. Vail walked up to Sharp as he wanted to know what he had encountered and experienced.

"What did you come across?"

"I came across a spirit that did not want to leave." Vail said. "However, he had no choice. He had his time in the world of the living, its time he entered the world of the dead."

"So, is the place safer to live in?"

Vail paused and looked back at the mansion.

"As long as they don't bother with the burial ground or bring in any type of spiritual items that may invoke a spirit, they should be just fine."

"Sharp extended his hand toward Vail.

"I thank you for coming and solving this problem." "Believe me, we really needed it."

"I just do what I must." Vail said.

Vail walked toward his vehicle that resembled a 1970s car. He drives away as the sun started to rise above the location of the mansion.

PRAYERS FOR THE DEAD

Occult detective and paranormal investigator Travis Vail has been called in to investigate a series of haunting events that have plagued an old-century church. The owners of the church have told Vail that it was once used as a place for satanic rituals by Satanists. Vail understands the power that Satanists tamper with and what they can release if not careful. Along with Vail on this investigation is Dr. Galen Donovan, a middle-aged African American who's well-practiced in the fields of exorcism and paranormal investigation.

Dr. Donovan arrived at the abandoned church to speak with the current priest. As they talked and discussed the series of haunting that have taken place, Vail entered the church, walking inside calmly while observing the interior. Dr. Donovan stood up from his seat and walked toward Vail.

"Detective Travis Vail, it's an honor to meet you." Donovan said.

"Same here, Doctor." Vail replied. "I hear you're going to be investigating the church with me."

"I am. I feel it's better to do mainly because of my history with exorcisms."

"Just in case I end up being partially possessed supposedly, you'll find a way to help me." Vail said.

"Exactly."

Vail nodded.

"Fair enough then."

Vail walked over to the priest, greeting one another as they shook hands. The priest escorted Vail and Donovan throughout the church.

Walking through the church, Vail noticed some distinctive red smears on the walls. He asked the priest about them. The priest had responded by saying those markings are the previous locations where pentagrams were once painted. The smears were done by wiping them off the walls. Donovan shook his head, rubbing his chin.

"They really chose a place like this to do their worshipping." Donovan questioned.

"Tell me, these folks have to be led by someone." Vail said. "Any idea as to where their leader could've gone?"

"Their leader hasn't been seen for some time." The priest responded. "We hope to find him.

"Surely you will."

The Priest continued to walk them through the church. Vail looked at the site and studied every room inside. Donovan thanked the Priest for showing them around and for allowing them to investigate the haunting. After saying thanks, Vail traveled to the nearest museum to do some extra research concerning Satanism and the Occult. Once he had studied the arts of both. He discovered that the cult's leader might be lurking around the surrounding land of the church.

Upon returning to the church, with Donovan at his side, the sun started to set as they enter the church. The Priest said a prayer for them before he left. Vail and Donovan looked around the silent church, walking through the chapel and passing through the pews. Donovan told Vail to be very careful and to watch his surroundings. Vail turned to him, looking prepared.

"I did some research of my own to prepare for this night."

"Hope you put it to good use."

"I will."

Vail looked ahead of him and seen something glowing underneath some of the pews. Vail looked closer, squinting his eyes and what he seen were two red eyes in the distance. He ran after it, Donovan startled and followed. Vail ran through the aisle between the pews, chasing the red eyes. Vail stopped at the podium, not seeing the eyes anywhere. Donovan caught up to him, looking around as well.

"What did you see?"

"Two red eyes." Vail said. "Very distinctive."

"They're here now."

Vail walked down the left hall of the chapel, passing through the other offices. As Donovan followed, he heard a distinct voice in the distance of the hall that sounded like a woman calling him.

"I just heard a voice."

"Did it sound like a woman or a child?"

"It was a woman's voice. She was calling to me."

"I'm sure you're aware not to follow that voice. Could be a demon mimicking a woman to lure you into a trap."

"Of course."

Vail heard the same female voice coming from the end

of the hall. He is tempted to follow due to its high pitch sound. Spotting the two red eyes again with a laughing sound. He chases after it again. Donovan is quickly able to follow Vail this second time.

Entering another room that appears to be a lobby area, Vail stopped Donovan as they both saw the full apparition of a demonic entity. It appeared as a female, but Vail noticed the horns coming from its head, only to be seen by its shadow against the stone wall.

Donovan pulled out a cross at aimed it at the demon. It slowly backed up against the wall and started to laugh. Once, Donovan took a few steps back, the demon vanished. Vail turned to Donovan, noticing that the cross barely worked. Vail took out a bottle of holy water. He also took out his small notepad, re-reading what he had wrote down in the museum regarding demons.

They continued to walk through the church with only six hours left before sunrise. Getting no responses of any kind. They stumbled upon a red pentagram painted on the wooden floor. Vail glances more closely at the symbol and turned to Donovan.

"It's still wet and its blood."

Donovan kneeled, looking at the symbol. He told Vail that the blood is indeed what he feared, human blood. He took a sample of the blood for further testing. Vail put his hand over the symbol. He felt the sense of heat coming from it, intense heat.

"Whoever put this here knows what they were doing and have summoned up something."

"What could they have possibly summoned? More demons? More malevolent entities?"

Vail slowly looked around him and Donovan and

glanced at the pentagram.

"One thing. You would think the person who placed this here would still be inside this church."

"Certainly."

They suddenly hear footsteps behind them in the distance. From the sound, they appear to be coming closer. Vail and Donovan slowly turned around as the steps became loud enough for the echoes to become silent. As they turn, they see a man wearing a black trench coat with all black clothing. The man has long wavy black hair.

"Who are you, fellow?" Vail asked.

"Vernon Lance."

Donovan looked at Lance and started to take a few steps toward him. Pointing at him with a question in mind.

"I get the sense that you're responsible for the pentagram on the floor."

"Indeed I am. I'm the cult's Priest."

"Using human blood! What kind of man does such a thing?"

"A greater kind. One needs the blood of a human to gain knowledge of the hidden power that surrounds us all."

"He's the one responsible for all of this. The demonic haunting, the previous pentagrams that covered the interior of this church."

"I understand that average people such as yourselves couldn't fully understand to have taken this course to bring about the next civilization."

Donovan stared.

"Quickly, Vail!"

Vail quickly pulled out his notepad, setting up to recite a ritual to Lance. Donovan took out a bottle of holy water, preparing to toss it at Lance. Lance looked unworried about his current circumstance.

"I don't know why you're preparing to attack me. I'm only human with demonic intellect."

"We're not going to attack you, we're condemning you." Vail said.

"You're ready?' Donovan said.

"I am."

Vail began to recite the pagan ritual as he stared into Lance's piercing green eyes with Donovan preparing to toss the holy water into Lance's face. Lance stood his ground with his arms standing upward, open for Vail and Donovan's attacks. Lance smiled at Vail and Donovan.

"It's really taking a while for you two to finish your condemning."

"Shut your mouth!" Vail said.

Donovan glanced at Vail, knowing Lance's distraction is causing Vail's ritual to cease working.

"Vail, his distraction is ceasing the ritual."

"That can't be possible." Vail remarked.

Lance grinned.

"Anything is possible in this universe to be maneuvered. Besides, I have to say it again, I am human with demonic intellect."

"What can we do now?" Vail said to Donovan.

Lance quickly raised his arm above his head, covering his face from the light coming through the window. Vail and Donovan notice Lance's strange behavior and turn around, seeing the sun rise and its light causing Lance to hide. Vail turned around and Lance has disappeared. Donovan notices burn marks on the ground where Lance was previously standing. The marks are still burning as if Lance was pulled into the ground by an unknown force of energy.

An hour later, the priest returned to the church, seeing Vail and Donovan standing and waiting in the chapel, sitting on the back pews. The priest walked up to them both, shaking their hands.

"Appears you two have had quite an investigation."

"We did."

Vail pulled out his notepad, revealing that he had wrote down Lance's name and description. He showed the priest as he told him about their investigation and how they later ran into Lance. Vail also tells the priest that Lance suddenly vanished as the sun rose and its light shined through into the room. The priest thanked them for their investigation of the church.

As they walked off, Donovan told the priest that they will have someone to come over and clean the pentagram off the floor and give a cleansing of the room to avoid any contact with demonic entities and to close to possible portal that may lie inside the room.

Vail walked to his car as Donovan approached him.

"It was a pleasure to work with you, Travis Vail."

"Likewise, here, Doctor. Hopefully we can work together again."

"I'm highly sure we will."

They shook hands as Vail gets into his car and drives off the location and down the road. Donovan looked around the surrounding areas of the church to find any further evidence of Lance's disappearance. Donovan discovers a track of burn marks within the grass. He followed the tracks as they lead him to an open field. Within the field, Donovan noticed a marking on the ground. The marking

was an enlarged pentagram carved into the field that was
large enough for a small home to fit in.

<u>A LOST GIRL</u>

In the suburbs of Chesterfield, New Hampshire, Cooper and Janice Lawrence have contacted Travis Vail to investigate mysterious behavior of their nine-year old daughter, Carrie Lawrence. According to the parents, Carrie had been participating in some unusual behavior, talking and playing with an imaginary friend whom she calls Leta. Within a few days, Carrie began to act a certain behavior that appeared to be abnormal to her parents, speaking in an unknown tongue and drawing art that seemed to have an infatuation with death and fire.

Vail arrived at the suburb home of the Lawrence family. He walked toward the door and knocked three times. Cooper opened the door and greeted Vail, allowing him to enter his home. When Vail walked inside the home, he immediately felt a negative presence. He looked around the home's first room, which was a living room, next to a kitchen. Sitting on the couch in the living room watching TV is Carrie.

"Carrie, meet Mr. Vail." Janice said.

Carrie turned and looked at Vail. She stared at him for

quite a bit before turning back toward the TV. Vail turned to Cooper and Janice. He asked them about Carrie's behavior when she began to speak about an imaginary friend. Janice told him that it stared when Carrie went outside to play with some neighbors before she saw a young girl sitting by a tree, who she claimed to be Leta. Vail told them that he will investigate their home later that night to find evidence of Carrie's friend.

Vail returned to their home and began his investigation. Upon finding no source that could trace to Carrie's imaginary friend. He started to doubt that he would find anything related to Leta. Though, Vail walked into the backyard to the site where Carrie came into contact with Leta. Vail noticed some form of objects buried in the dirt by the tree. What Vail found was a locket necklace. Inside the locket was a photo of a young girl with the name Leta under the photo. Vail took the locket and left the home, stating that more research had to be done.

The next day, Vail meets with Raynard Brown, a historian. Raynard greets Vail as he pulls out the locket and showed the picture. Raynard looked at the photo.

"I would like to see if you could tell me what century this photo was taken in?"

"Appears it dates to the late 19th century."

"The late 1800s you say."

"Indeed. Tell me, what about this picture intrigues you, Mr. Vail?"

"I'm currently on an investigation about a young girl's imaginary friend. This locket was buried by a tree where the girl first met the imaginary friend."

"So, I take it, you believe this young girl on the photo is the imaginary friend?"

"That's my current guess. Even though, when I walked into the home, I felt a negative presence that seemed beyond human."

"It is possible that a demon could have taken the form of this "*Leta*" and is using it to deceive and control the young girl."

Raynard handed the locket back to Vail, who placed it inside his coat pocket.

"I'm heading back over there immediately to do another form of test."

"Wish you luck on this one."

"Thanks, but I'm not an actual believer in luck."

Vail left the building, returning to the suburb home of the Lawrence Family.

Vail returned to the home, he sat with Cooper and Janice to speak with them about Carrie. Janice request for Carrie to sit in her room while they talk with Vail. Carrie walked into her room and closed the door. Cooper turned to Vail.

"So, what have you discovered so far?"

"I found this buried in your backyard." Vail said, pulling out the locket from his coat pocket.

Vail handed the locket to them. Cooper opened it and seen the picture of a little girl. Janice placed her hand over her mouth as she saw the name "Leta" beneath the picture. Cooper pointed.

"That's the name which Carrie told us. That's the name of her friend."

"So, you're telling us this is who Carrie's been talking with?" asked Janice with fear in her voice.

"It's a possible theory. Not sure so far since I would like

to speak with Carrie, if you don't mind."

"Sure."

Janice called out Carrie to sit with them. Carrie sat between her parents as she stared at Vail. Looking him in the eyes. Vail could feel the heavy presence from her.

"Carrie, I would like to ask you about your friend, Leta."

"She doesn't like you."

"How can you tell?"

"She told me that you're here to get rid of her. She says you won't be able to because we're friends."

"I know you're just a child, you shouldn't play around with things you can't comprehend."

"I understand enough, thanks to Leta."

Janice turned to Cooper, frightened at her daughter's words toward Vail. Cooper looked at his daughter, worried about her well-being.

"Honey, what has Leta told you?"

"Leta told me that we will be friends forever and no one can breakup our friendship. Not even this man here."

"Sweetie, this man is here to help you." Janice told her daughter.

"This man is here to ruin my friendship with Leta and I won't let him."

"Carrie, me and your mother have decided that you cannot be friends with Leta anymore."

"Leta is my friend and we will always be together. Whether any of you like it or not."

Vail looked into Carrie's eyes and noticed a slight change. Her eyes had shifted solid black for a quick second. He warned Cooper and Janice of this change and told them to stay guard of what could possibly happen.

"Carrie, where is Leta at this moment?"

"She's here with us."

Vail stood up and looked around the room, Cooper and Janice looked around, but saw nothing. They looked at their daughter with fear and confusion, not understanding what is happening to her.

"What is she doing?"

"She's plotting to kill you silly." Carrie said with a smile.

Carrie giggled as objects in the room began to levitate and throw themselves at Vail. He ducked the thrown objects that came his way. He yells to Cooper and Janice to take Carrie out of the house. They take Carrie and leave the home in a hurry. Vail is left inside the house by himself, seeing the objects in the room levitating and moving around with no natural explanation. Vail knew it was Leta's doings.

"Leta, I know it's you. If you wanted a fight, you have one with me."

The objects ceased moving and the room quickly turned silent. Vail slowly walked through the house, with a ritual notebook in his hands, equipped with a metal cross.

"Where are you, Leta? I know you're still inside this house."

Vail heard a set of footsteps coming from behind him. The footsteps become louder as Vail stood his guard. He turned to see what could be creating the footsteps and when he turned around, he sees Carrie's room and coming from the room is a young girl, the same girl from the photo. She is Leta.

"So, you're Leta."

"I am. Who are you supposed to be?"

"I'm Travis Vail, occult detective. My job is to find and solve cases that involve the paranormal, such as you."

"There's no reason for you to have ever come here. We were doing just fine before you came into our lives."

"First off, you don't have a life anymore. You're dead. Secondly, you're turning a young girl into a monster. Her parents are scared to death of their daughter because of your influence."

"Her parents are a thing of the past. Carrie is the future and I'm guiding her in the right direction."

"You're not guiding her in any direction but the paths of pain and death. You don't belong in this world anymore, Leta."

"What gives you the right to say so?"

"Because it's my purpose."

Vail took out the cross and held it toward Leta. She slowly backed away from Vail, her hands up, covering her face and screaming at him to drop the cross.

"I'm not dropping it." Vail stated.

Leta looked at Vail and smiled. She waived her hand toward the cross and it melted in Vail's hands. Turning into liquid ash. Vail stepped back, looking down at the remains of the cross.

"You know that stuff doesn't work on us." Leta smirked.

Vail had realized Leta isn't an ordinary ghost who's trapped on Earth. She is the negative energy that he felt, and he now knows she's a demonic entity posing as the young girl in the picture.

"What are you going to do, Spirit-Seeker?" Leta inquired. "Show me what you have to offer."

"It's time for you to go, little demon."

"You have no understanding. I'm not going anywhere!"

Leta raised her hand, causing a wave of energy to hit Vail. The wave was powerful enough to pick Vail off the ground and knocking him into a wall. He looked up and doesn't see Leta anywhere.

"This girl I tell you." Vail muttered to himself as he stood up.

Cooper and Janice walked back into the house with Carrie. Entering, they see the living room covered with shattered frames, vases, and other objects on the ground. Vail walked back into the room, seeing Cooper, Janice, and Carrie.

"Are you alright?" Janice said.

"I'm alright. Why did you come back inside?"

"We heard noises going on and we wanted to see what was happening." Cooper said.

"What did you find?" Janice asked.

"For starters, I seen your daughter's imaginary friend. She's a tough one to deal with."

"You're telling us that Carrie's friend isn't imaginary, but real."

"That's what I'm telling you. She wants the two of you to stay out of her way. She said she's influencing Carrie for the future."

"Influencing her? There's nothing wrong with our daughter."

"I thoroughly believe that your daughter is mildly possessed by Leta. That would explain the shifting eyes and her friend coming from her room"

"Why do we have to go through this." Janice stammered.

"Lot of people have these problems in a lot of different

ways. I'm just here to help out."

Janice grabbed Vail's hand, looking him in the eyes with fear. Vail could feel her fear.

"You have to save our daughter. You must."

Vail nodded. Cocked his head with a nod and slight chuckle.

"I have one more solution that can be done."

"Name it."

"I'll have to exorcize your home and your daughter."

Later at nightfall, Carrie is sitting down on the couch in between her parents. Vail walked into the room with holy water. He dabs his thumb into the water and created an insignia onto Carrie's forehead. She screamed as the first touch of water burned her. Her parents held her tightly during the burning sensation that she felt.

"That confirmed she is mildly possessed." Vail said. "Thought you should know that. For the best."

"What are you going to do next?" Cooper asked.

"Read a ritual that will lift the essence of Leta from your daughter and send her to the other side."

Vail took out his book of rituals and began reciting the ritual of lifting Leta's essence. The home was quiet and there weren't any sounds to be heard.

"I, Travis Vail, read from the book of rituals, I hereby declare a cleansing of this home and its inhabitants."

Carrie started to shake, as if she was losing control of her body. Her parents held her down as Vail continued to do the ritual.

"I hereby command the spirit of Leta to leave this home and its inhabitants."

Vail looked at Carrie as she screamed in pain. Janice's face covered with tears as she held her daughter down.

Cooper held in his emotions. Carrie looked at Vail with intense anger, now knowing that it isn't Carrie.

"You'll never take me away from here!" Carrie said with a changed voice. A deep-pitched voice.

"We'll see about that." Vail replied.

Vail continued reciting as black smoke started to emit from the house and from Carrie into the air. Vail ran over to the door and opened it as the black smoke swiftly flew out of the house. Carrie stopped screaming and fell unconscious. Janice called out to her for a response. The smoke left the home and Carrie. Vail shut the door and approached the parents.

"There's nothing to worry about. She's fine."

"Thank you." Cooper said.

"Thank you so much." Janice beamed.

Vail prepared himself to leave the home and was getting himself ready. Before he left, he was stopped by Janice, who hugged him for his help. Cooper stood behind Janice, smiling.

"Thank you again."

"It's my job to help."

"If I may ask, where did the spirit go?" Cooper inquired.

"Leta went to a place that she will feel comfortable, I hope. In truth, she was just a lost girl looking for a way out."

Vail left the neighborhood and Carrie awoke inside her room with her parents over here, smiling.

"What happened, mommy?"

"It's a long story."

LOCKED FOR ETERNITY

Travis Vail has decided to investigate a century year-old prison. The prison is called Desdemona Penitentiary. Its inner structure is surrounded with over thirteen cell blocks across acres of land. There have been notable deaths throughout the prison and through its existence. From murders, to raping, to riots, and suicides, there is no doubt that there are entities that reside within the prison walls.

Vail arrived at the prison, which is located on the east coast of London. Colton Levi, a close friend of Vail's comes to the prison's entrance. He joined Vail for the investigation as they are greeted by the owner of the prison and its land, Robert Leonard. A man in his middle age.

"You've finally made it here, Mr. Vail"

"I'm honored you've contacted me about this place. I've heard many stories throughout time."

"Who's the partner?"

"He's Colton Levi. One of my closest friends within the field."

"I take it he won't be afraid of what's inside."

"He shouldn't be. He's done this before in many

places."

"Those places weren't Desdemona, my friend."

Leonard opened the gated entrance to the prison. They walked through the front yard, noticing gravestones that stand in a field on the side of the prison. Levi took out his camera, he began taking pictures of the outer structure of the prison and the gravestones. Leonard pointed toward the gravestones.

"Those stones belong to some of the prisoners that died here."

"I notice there's no names on them." Vail mentioned. "Just only numbers."

"Their prison numbers. Didn't matter what their names were. They were called by their six-digit prison numbers."

"That's a terrible thing. I suspect they're not at rest." Levi said.

"They aren't' They're still here in these walls."

They entered the prison, looking at its intense inner structure. Vail looked around, seeing many cells toward them. Levi continues to take pictures. Leonard walked them over to three cells. He tells them that's where many soldiers from World War I were kept after the war was over. Levi took pictures of the interior of the cells. He looked at one and noticed a black smog hovering off the ground. Levi was shaking, but calm.

"Vail, I think I found something already."

Levi showed Vail the photo, seeing the black smog inside the second cell. Vail walked inside the cell, standing in the middle, quiet and calm. Leonard and Levi stood outside the door, watching Vail.

"Whoever decided to manifest themselves as a black smog, I suggest you tell us your name and place, now."

Getting no response, Leonard continued to take them around the prison. They walked through different halls of the prison.

"The first cell block was famously known for murders."

"How many murders exactly?" Vail asked.

"Estimated over six hundred. At least."

"That's a lot of death and anger." Levi said.

"That's right. The second cell block areas is known for the large amount of rapes that took place."

"You're saying male prisoners raped other male prisoners?" Vail said.

"There were female prisoners, visitors, and minor female officers. So, it's possible they were the targets."

"Of course."

Leonard walked by the last few cells and pointed down the halls.

"Suicides apparently dominated this entire area."

"It seems each cell block carries its own kind of death." Vail said. "If you wanted to be murdered, you have the first section. If you wanted to be raped, you had the second section. Now, if you wanted to kill yourself, you had the third section."

"Choose your own fate, basically." Leonard said.

"They chose it well I suppose." Levi said.

After seeing much of the prison. Vail traveled to the nearest library to read up on more history of the prison. Levi went on an errand to gather a pair of digital cameras, digital recorders, and EMP device to catch frequency energy signatures. Finding the library, Vail discovered the origin of the prison. It was founded by a well-known millionaire during the late 1800s.

The prison was first used as a correctional facility for

juveniles and over the years became a penitentiary during the start of World War I. Both during and after World War I, many of the soldiers, from either side were kept within the prison. The prison continued to stand even after World War II and the Vietnam War. It was used briefly during the height of the Cold War. Vail read on how the prison was shut down in 2003 due to low funding.

Vail returned to the prison with Levi, who was carrying the bags of the digital supplies. Vail looked at Levi and took a glance at the bags. He smirked.

"You love your technology."

"How else are we able to capture images and video of spirits."

Leonard walked out of the prison towards Vail and Levi. They walk back inside the prison as Leonard closes the gate as the sun sets. Vail looked back at Leonard and nodded. Leonard nodded back in respect.

"Hope you find what you're looking for."

"Don't worry, we will."

Levi began to set up the digital cameras on tripods across the hallways of the cell blocks. Vail recited a ritual that is known to protect both himself and Levi from malevolent spirits that may reside inside the prison walls. Vail approached Levi, who's finished setting up the cameras and recorders.

"You're ready for this?" Vail asked.

"How can I not be ready for this."

Once the moon glinted across the prison windows, Vail and Levi started their investigation. They first decided to check the first six cell blocks. They stood inside of the circular shaped room, seeing all the entrances of the cell blocks, Levi looked around as he noticed something familiar about the circular room.

"This place is a smorgasbord of spirits."

"You know, Vail, this room reminds me of another prison in the states. I've seen it on one of the paranormal shows."

"I hope they did a good job."

"They did. One of the best paranormal shows on TV to date."

They slowly walk through the prison. Levi, with a digital camera in his hands, looks around through the LED screen as Vail uses his senses to track his location.

"You want to start the conversations?" Vail said.

"Sure."

Levi walked by the cells and stood in front of the fourth one. He pointed the camera towards the cell, looking inside, seeing the bed spring, sink, and toilet. Vail walked towards the other cells nearby.

"Is there anyone inside this cell?" Levi said. "We want to know if you're here or not."

"They're here, Levi. Just be careful."

Walking slowly and calm through the darkness of the cell block, they began to hear sounds of knocking coming from the cell blocks.

Levi looked around with his camera at the cells, seeing nothing in the lens. Vail entered a few of the cells.

"Are you in here? If you are, I demand you say or do something now."

The knocking increased as Levi spotted a shadow that walked by the cell where Vail was standing inside of. Levi ran over toward the cell, telling Vail what he captured on the camera and how it passed by the cell he was standing in. Vail left the cell and continued to investigate the other cells.

"So, more deaths took place in this cell block." Levi mentioned. "The other guys would've loved to see this."

"I'm sure they would. Over six-hundred murders in this location. That's a lot of energy."

While walking toward the end of the cell block, Vail caught a shadow, which moved past the exit door. He looked back to see it, but nothing was there. Levi noticed Vail's behavior.

"What is it?" Levi asked.

"I saw a shadow. It walked past the exit."

"Let me try the digital recorder to capture their voice."

Levi pulled out the digital recorder. He talked into it, asking a series of questions to the spirits within the cell block. After a minute to a second, he received a response. Vail walked over and listened to the recorder. He hears the voice of an older man, threatening to kill them if they don't leave the cell block.

"It just threatened to kill us." Levi remarked.

"It can't kill us if it doesn't have enough energy to use. Don't lend them your energy. Block it all off. That includes the devices."

"I'll try."

"You will. There's no trying in here. We're in dangerous territory right now."

Upon getting no other signs of spirits within the cell block. They entered the second area of the cell block. While they walked in, they could hear disembodied screams coming from the cells. Levi looked around cautiously.

"You hear those screams, Vail?"

"They sound like women in pain."

"They're being raped!" Levi yelled.

"It could be just an irrelevant response. A sound that

was once here repeating itself."

"We have to check to be sure."

"I am sure it's an irrelevant spirit."

Levi walked over to the cells, seeing no one inside. He looked through the camera to find anything. Seeing nothing, they walk further down the cell block. As they walked through the cell block, they heard a distant laugh coming from the left of them. Vail walked by the cells on the left, looking inside.

"Who's here with us?" Vail asked. "I demand you give us a response of your presence."

Across from Vail, a small rock is thrown toward him from the cell block. Levi scouted and found the small rock on the floor nearby Vail's area. He looked around, showing minor signs of fear while Vail was calm and quiet.

"You want to throw things at us now. I see you want to play rough. We can play rough."

"What are you talking about, Vail? They just threw a rock at you."

"I've went up against worse than a small pebble."

Vail walked around the cell block. They began hearing more screams and laughs. Levi started to shiver as he sweated and stood against a corner. Vail stood in the middle of the cell block, both arms at his side, with no expression on his face.

"They're playing with us, Colton. We're in their territory."

"They're playing kind of tough." Levi muttered.

The screams and laughs had silenced, leaving the cell block to become completely silent. Vail told Levi that they're going to the third and last section of the cell blocks. They entered the third section, feeling their energy being drained and feeling signs of dizziness. They started to feel depressed as they could hear crying within the cell block.

"What's going on?" Levi asked. "I starting to feel drained and dizzy."

"They're using our energy to fill themselves up. That crying might be the start of it."

The crying continued as they walk through the cell block. Still feeling drained and dizzy, they looked around, seeing shadowed, disembodied figures walking around them. Levi tried to hold the camera up to capture the shadow figures. As he captured them on the camera, the camera froze and completely shut down, signaling the sign of a low battery.

"I just charged this camera." Levi shouted.

"They're using its energy." Vail said. "They're gathering as much as they need."

"So, what do we do?"

"We use our instinct to see and to touch. Not all the spirits are intelligent or benevolent. I'm starting to sense a malevolent spirit in here and it doesn't belong in this cell block."

"They're jumping cell blocks now." Levi blurted.

Vail felt a presence surrounding him closely. He could feel something on his back, he knew they were hands. The presence of the hands shoved him violently against the wall. Levi looked and went to help him up. Vail scanned the cell block, still dizzy and drained from losing energy. He continued to walk through the cell block and stood upon staring at a black smog. Levi also saw the smog and he pointed toward it.

"That's what I saw earlier on the camera."

"That's not a benevolent spirit. Its malevolent and

belongs in the murder cell block.”

The black smog didn’t move. It only stood still in the air. Vail and Levi continued to stare at it. Vail reached into his coat pocket, taking out the book of rituals. Levi looked over at the book seeing the variety of rituals inside.

“What are you about to do?”

“I’m about to send this spirit to the other side. Where it can be judged for its sins.”

Vail recited the ritual, making a way to send the malevolent spirit to the other side. As he recited the ritual, the black smog slowly evaporated before vanishing into the thin air. Vail looked around, not seeing any more shadow figures. Levi rubbed his head.

“I’m not dizzy anymore.” Levi said.

“Neither am I. The ritual must have sent them over.”

Vail looked toward the window above them, seeing the sunlight peeking through the cracks into the cell block. He and Levi walked toward the entrance. Levi gathered the tripods and cameras that sat in the hallways. Leonard returned as the morning started and thanked them for their investigation.

“So, may I ask what you seen or heard?”

“We heard a lot and seen a lot.” Levi said.

“There are many spirits that reside in this place. I would only believe that they’re locked in for eternity because of the path they chose to go.”

“I believe that very well. I guess they’ll never find a way out of here.”

“They’ll find a way to leave and enter the other side. It will take some time of course for it to be done.”

“Well, I want to thank you for coming over here and investigating this place. Not many would have done this.”

"It's what we're here for."

Vail signaled to Levi to leave. Levi places the cameras and devices in the back of the car before getting in the passenger's set as Vail drives away from the prison.

CASE OF THE WHITE LADY

Travis Vail is set to investigate Huntly Castle where legends speak of a spirit known as The White Lady resides. Vail had read up on the history of the White Lady and how she is involved with Huntly Castle. After arriving in the country of Scotland, Vail traveled to *Aberdeenshire*, one of the thirty-two council areas within Scotland. Aberdeenshire is also a lieutenancy area. As Vail arrived in Aberdeenshire, he traveled straight for Huntly Castle. Once on Huntly Castle's land, he started at the castle, scanning its structure as a twelve-century castle.

A man walked from the castle, he greeted Vail as they stood outside the historic structure. The man is Barclay Iomhair, the current tour guide and owner of Huntly Castle's property. Vail speaks with Barclay about the castle and its history. Barclay tells him that the castle was built by Clan Gordon in the twelfth century as an L-Plan tower house. Vail began to ask about the castle's former inhabitants as Barclay tells him about how it was formally named *Strathbogie* and how it was granted to Sir Adam Gordon of Huntly in the fourteenth century.

He told Vail that the castle was once burned down and later rebuilt. They begin to walk through the interior of the castle, seeing all its ancient structure around them. Vail states that he can feel the emotions of the people that once lived in the castle. Barclay begins to tell him about the well-known folklore that travels around the castle. The folklore of the White Lady. Vail turned to Barclay, he showed a slight smirk.

"I'm curious about this folklore." Vail said. "What's the exact tale of this White Lady?"

"There are many tales of the White Lady to be exact according to my knowledge."

Barclay began to tell Vail about the case of a daughter of the Lyon Family. He tells him how she committed a folly that everyone else thought was heinous and how a male servant was involved in the folly. He tells Vail the daughter was banished to a bedchamber in the tower of the castle, which was believed to be over one hundred feet from the ground. He says she suffered from agony within her mind and later found relief from either jumping or pushed out of the tower's window and fell to her death. He continued saying the tale was passed from each generation that came afterwards. The room where she was banished to is now known as the Waterloo Room.

The second tale is the most well-known tale of the White Lady and how it's about the Countess of Strathmore who had entered her second ill marriage. Barclay tells Vail that the Countess has suffered greatly within the romance part of her life as she lived unhappy with the husbands who later turned another way. She wrote about her experiences as being wretched and her writing is still described today as the most damning indictment of a husband ever to be written by a wife in any age.

Barclay decided to tell Vail that the most-well known one is on the halfway of being the accurate story as he believes the Lyon daughter is the White Lady that haunts the castle. Vail tells Barclay he'll surely discover who the White Lady truly is during his investigation. Vail leaves Huntly Castle and heads toward a nearby library, where he will look up more of the castle's history and residents. He finds records of the castle being burned down and how King James IV of Scotland would come over and gave gifts to the stonemasons that worked on the castle. He also reads that in October of 1503, King James IV returned to play a shooting contest and later came the Huntly Castle every October after as part of an annual pilgrimage to the shrine of Saint Duthac of Tain, a royal bough and post town in the Highland area of Scotland.

Vail retuned to the castle grounds just before sunset as he spoke with Barclay. Knowing he couldn't be locked in for the whole night, he decided to stay on the castle grounds from sunset to sunrise. Barclay leaves the area as Vail stood and stared at Huntly Castle. He decided to walk around the area for a while until the sun had set. He examines the area twice as the sun starts to set. Smirking, while watching the sunset. He begins his investigation of Huntly Castle.

"The sun has set, and I am here on Huntly Castle ground. I am here to see the White Lady."

He walked through the ruined structure of the castle, calling out the legendary White Lady. Not receiving any sign of her in his presence, he continues his investigation. Upon walking through the ruined castle, he spotted a white mist moving from right to left in the darker parts of the castle. Vail takes out a flashlight and approaches the darker area.

"Who is here with me? I would like for you, whoever you are, to make some sort of contact with me, so that I know you're here."

Vail entered the dark area, not able to see anything in front of him without the flashlight. He begins to hear a distant cry coming from inside the dark area. Vail looked around the entire area, not able to see what the crying was coming from. He could still hear it while looking around the entire area. He does a double take around the area. Still seeing nothing, he decides to leave the area. As he approached the front of the castle, he sees a young boy dressed in a double-breasted sailing jacket. Vail approached the young boy slowly, staring into his eyes.

"What's your name, son?" Vail said. "You can tell me your name."

The boy gave no response to Vail. Vail continues to ask the boy about his name as the boy stayed quiet. After one last attempt to get a response from the boy, he walks away. Vail watched as the boy slowly faded away as he was walking away. Vail says to himself that he just seen a spirit, but it wasn't the legendary White Lady that locals and folklore speak of. The sun begins to rise as Vail takes one look back at Huntly Castle before leaving Aberdeenshire.

The next day, Vail traveled to *Longforgan*, Perth and Kinross in Scotland. He traveled through Longforgan to find a prison that's known as Castle Huntly. Sort of the sane title as the ruined castle in Aberdeenshire. While during research the day before, Vail discover documents containing information about a fifteen-century year old castle with Huntly as a name. Like the other castle, this Huntly is currently an HM prison. HM stands for His Majesty's Prison.

Vail arrived at the prison castle, looking at its structure and seeing how it's been renovated and adapted to stay in modern times. Upon entering the prison, he discovers it's an open prison, with the capacity of two-hundred and eighty-five people. Not sure about how he could do an investigation throughout the prison, he decides to find a way. After speaking with officials within the prison and some of the prisoners themselves, he discovers that the White Lady has also been seen in the prison, including the same young boy that was seen at the ruined Huntly Castle.

Later that night, Vail decides to do a minimal investigation throughout the prison. He decided to leave two hours after midnight to avoid the prisoners. Once his investigation started, he began to hear prisoners screaming across the hallways. He ran down the hallways to find the prisoners. Once at the end, he sees prisoners staring at a woman, who's floating in the air. She's only wearing white with white hair and clear glowing white eyes.

"It has to be her." Vail said.

The prisoners run in opposite directions to avoid the lady. Vail walked up to the lady as she slowly turned toward him. They lock eyes as Vail has officially come face to face with the White Lady. Vail smirked as he stared at her. Her face showed no emotion as she continues to stare him down. Other prisoners look from across the hallways, staring at Vail and the White Lady.

"So, you the legendary White Lady." Vail said. "After all this time, I've finally got the chance to meet you."

The White Lady says nothing to respond to Vail. He continued to talk to her as the prisoners continued to hide across the hallways. Vail decided to reach into his pocket and take out his book of rituals. The White Lady glanced at the book, noticing its symbolic encryptions on the front and back. She vanished in seconds as Vail looked around, not seeing her anywhere.

"Dammit."

Vail ran through the hallways searching for the White Lady. As he went through each hall, he continued to only see prisoners standing or sitting down. He stopped to take a breath and he started to hear what sounded like prisoners fighting each other down the hall he just past. Vail returned to that hall and seen the prisoners fighting each other as the White Lady went passed them in seconds. Vail followed the white trail of mist that was made by the White Lady.

He continued to search for the White Lady as it was only thirty minutes before he left the prison. He walked into a room that resembled a museum of the castle's history. As he walked slowly through the museum, he finds artifacts that date to the origin of the castle's existence. As he looked at the artifacts, he starts to notice the room's temperature lower. He pulled out a thermometer, which signified the room's temperature was below thirty degrees. He turned around, looking around the museum. Vail raised up his left sleeve and looked at his arm, noticing the hairs standing up completely straight.

"I know you're here." Vail uttered. "You can come on out, so we can discuss your place in the future."

Vail feels a swift breeze on the back of his neck. He

turned and sees the White Lady. She's standing on the ground, facing Vail. Vail stared at her, looking unworried about his possible safety. He glanced at his watch, seeing he only had fifteen minutes before his investigation was over.

"I only have fifteen minutes to help you before I leave this place." Vail said. "So, I am here to help you move on to the other side."

The White Lady shakes her head, disagreeing with Vail's wishes. Vail slowly reached into his pocket for his book. The Lady moved an inch closer to Vail. He stopped moving his hand and stared.

"I am here to help you, miss. There's no reason for you to stay in this place. Especially in today's time."

"You can't help me." The White Lady said. "You can even help yourself."

"Please, let me read from this book and I can send you to a better place. A wholesome place."

The White Lady giggled at Vail. He glanced at his watch and noticed he only had about ten minutes left before the investigation was over. He pulled out the book and turned to the page he was previously on before. The White Lady looked at the book.

"I only have about ten minutes left before I leave. I am sending you to the other side at this moment."

Vail read the ritual from the book as the White Lady tried to leave the room. In front of Vail, a white light shines through the entire room. The light begins to pull the Lady towards it as she begins to be pulled inside the light. The light later consumes her and vanishes. Vail placed the book back into his pocket and looked at the watch, seeing only six minutes left before he was done.

"There's nothing else for me to do here." Vail said.

Two hours after midnight, Vail leaves the prison castle. After the sun rose, he went back to Huntly Castle to speak with Barclay. Barclay sits inside his car as Vail approached him.

"I hear you visited Castle Huntly prison." Barclay said.

"I did."

"How was it? Going inside that place by yourself?"

"It was a worrisome task, but, I managed to get through it."

"So, I take it you saw something at both Huntly Castles?"

"I saw a young boy here. He vanished before I could get anything in place. At the prison is where I've seen the White Lady. It took a while before I could send her over to the other side to be in peace. It seemed to be that both places have been covered with the folklore of the White Lady."

Barclay smiled as Vail walked to his car.

"This means your case on this is officially done?"

"The case of the White Lady has been solved in my opinion."

Vail gets into his car before Barclay walked over to the car door,

"Give me a little insight on your next case?"

"I feel my next case will be in the States. Mostly to involve the legend of Salem."

Vail drove away as Barclay watched on.

SALEM WITCH TRIALS

Occult Detective Travis Vail has entered Salem, Massachusetts to investigate the historic tales of witchcraft and the possibility of it be continued in today's time. Salem is the key location to many historical accounts and records of witchcraft. The Salem Witch Trials took place between February 1692 and May 1693. Throughout the history of the years, paranoia and fear overtook Salem as many believed that The Devil was watching their every move. Anyone they saw or talked to that resemble unusual behavior was considered a witch or warlock.

Vail looked through the town of Salem. Knowing that it was a great effort to gain permission to investigate Salem's dark history. After a town council event, Vail was granted access to all of Salem and its historical records. Speaking with many of the town's residents, Vail realizes that witches still reside in Salem in modern day. Knowing they no longer hide and look just like the average person today. Vail traveled to the downtown area, asking many residents if they have seen any witches or if they are a witch themselves. Vail approaches two women wearing black cloaks, covering themselves from the cold light rain.

"If I may ask you ladies. Are any of you witches of modern day?"

"Why would you like to know? You're investigating the trials, aren't you?"

"Yes ma'am."

The women looked at each other and smirked. They turned toward Vail and shook their heads.

"I'll put to you this way, sir. Witches don't have a Jerusalem. They have Salem."

The women walked away, leaving Vail thinking about their last statement, saying how Salem is a witch's Jerusalem. Upon doing later research, Dr. Galen Donovan arrived in Salem and contacted Vail about his arrival. They later meet at the Lyceum restaurant, which sits on the land that once belonged to Bridget Bishop, the first woman who was hanged after being accused of practicing witchcraft.

"We're finally in Salem." Donovan said.

"It's been a long time coming. This one should be the one that's worth it."

"So, how was the town council meeting?"

"The meeting went great. Many residents agreed with what we're trying to do by discovering more evidence of their city's past and what truly happened."

"What's the current time that we head over to the Witch House?"

"Sometime this afternoon. I also plan to attend a play that resembles the trials exactly as the transcripts portray them. Once that's complete, we'll return to the house later tonight for the investigation."

Donovan nodded and looked down at his watch. Reading the time, he looked up toward Vail.

"Best we head over there at this moment."

"I agree."

Vail and Donovan arrived at the Salem Witch House. Looking at its old structure, Vail began to feel a chill coming from the house. Donovan noticed Vail's movement as if he's fighting something off.

"Is there something wrong, Vail?"

"I feel a presence of some kind. Not sure what it is, but it's coming from the house."

They approached the front door, being greeted by a woman named Fawn Verrucca. She greeted them as she allowed them inside the house. Once inside, they notice the historical artifacts the reside inside the rooms of the home.

"These are paintings that show the residents of this land. These are Elizabeth Gibbs' children. She had a total of four children. One of the children had died a year before she married Mr. Judge Jonathon Corwin. Her daughter, Margaret has passed away the second year she decided to get married."

"So, are all of these paintings portrayals of women?"

"Not these two on the wall."

Fawn pointed toward the wall, where two paintings were set. Vail bent down and looked at the paintings. He turned and looked at Donovan before facing Fawn.

"So, these two are paintings of young boys?"

"Yes, it is. They were known as Little Henry and Little Robert."

"So, they wore dresses in the late 1600s."

"Mainly until they reach around six years old. At least that age we know of."

"Fascinating." Donovan said. "You learn something new every day."

"If you have an open mind." Vail said. "So, what else can you tell us about this place?"

"Mr. Jonathon Corwin and the jury in the court had presided over the courses of the trials. Condemning many who were considered guilty, were put to death. Corwin even lived in this home."

"Was there a way that they could confess the truth to the jury, so they would be set free?" Donovan said.

"Their integrity was too prideful as they would rather die in this life and keep their integrity in the next. Instead of being what's considered a coward and just giving in to the Judge and jury's demands."

"So, this Bridget Bishop was one of the first women to be considered a witch." Vail said.

"She was first to be brought in as potentially being a witch due to her being an easy target. All the men would flirt with her as all the women would hate her and many of them condemned her as practicing witchcraft."

"So, this home belonged to Judge Corwin during those times of the trials?"

"Yes, it did. He lived in this very home."

"So, there should be much energy in this home." Vail said. "Maybe that explains what I was feeling before I entered."

"Also, in a way to find out if the women were witches, they would take their urine and mix it with flour, baking it into a cake. They would feed the cake to a dog and watch the dog for any unusual behavior or movements to determine if the women were witches."

"They fed dogs cake with urine baked in it." Donovan said. "Utterly disgusting."

"Horrifying at the most." Vail said.

Vail and Donovan later visited a location where they're going to watch a reenactment of the trials taken directly from the transcripts. As they enter the school, watching the young girls portray the historical figures of the witch trials. Donovan watches uncertainly with fear as Vail appeared to be in a trance, studying the words and movement of how the young girls portrayed the figures. After watching the reenactment, they decided to head back over to the Lyceum restaurant as they speak with residents who are currently sitting inside the restaurant. Vail and Donovan question as many as possible about Bridget Bishop. A few residents show Vail photos of a wedding that took place inside a banquet hall where in the photo is an apparition of a woman who they believe to be Bridget Bishop. After speaking with the residents, Vail noticed the sun is starting to set. He tells Donovan that they must head back over to the witch house to begin their investigation.

Once they returned to the witch house, Fawn allowed them back as she locked them within the home. Donovan began taking out equipment as Vail began to say a prayer over himself and Donovan, protecting them from any malevolent spirits that may reside inside the home or on the land itself.

"Much of the equipment is ready and set." Donovan said.

"I'll start once you're ready."

"I'm ready."

While Vail and Donovan walked into the living room of the home, Vain began to feel a chill as the room's temperature suddenly dropped. Donovan sees his own breath coming from his mouth. He turned over towards

Vail, who appeared to be fighting off something again.

"What's the problem?"

"I'm feeling someone else's emotions. I don't know who this is, but I am feeling a little sad for some reason and it's not my emotions."

"Are you going to be alright?"

"I'm not letting this get to me. But, I can't ignore what I'm feeling right now."

Donovan reached into his jacket pocket and pulled out an EMF Detector to find any EMF energy. Noting the major temperature drop, the EMF energy stops itself at the number "*666*".

"The energy is at "666"." Donovan said.

"What the hell is going on in here, Galen."

"We know there's something here with us right now."

Vail took out a digital recorder as Donovan walked around the home with the detector.

"Who's currently here with us? Mr. Donovan and I would like to know."

Donovan continued walking through the home with the detector.

"Find anything yet?" Vail said.

"Nothing yet. The temperature's back to normal."

Donovan suddenly felt hands on his back. He jumped up and turned toward Vail, who looked at him uncertainly.

"What's wrong?"

"I felt hands on my back."

"There's nothing behind you, Donovan. I'll check around this area to make sure what's around here."

Vail walked through the area of the room, using the digital recorder and asking questions towards the spirits. While asking the questions, he hears a disembodied female voice in the room he's currently inside. He turned quickly, scanning the room. Noticing Donovan inside the other room.

"Who's inside this room with me?"

He didn't get a response. A few hours later of not finding any signs of any spirit, Vail looked outside the window and seen the sun rising from behind the clouds. He turned to Donovan, who approached him with the other digital recorder and detector.

"The sun is rising." Vail said.

"Looks like this investigation is about over."

They packed up their gear and awaited Fawn to unlock the doors. Around 6:30 AM, Fawn arrived and unlocked the front doors, allowing Vail and Donovan to leave the house. Fawn, showing curiosity approached Vail as he began to enter his car.

"Did you discover anything?"

"Some uneasy feeling. Though, we must go through our recorders to make a perfect statement. Thank you for allowing us into this home."

Vail and Donovan leave the home as Fawn walked inside. She closed the door and through the window was an apparition of a female looking outside at Fawn as she left the house.

Within a few days, Vail and Donovan spent most of their time dissecting the recorders, searching for any signs of a spirit's voice. While scanning the recorders, Vail noticed a distinctive voice. He quickly paused and rewind the recorders, going back to the voice. Donovan approached him, looking at the screen.

"Find anything?"

"I believe I just did."

Vail played the audio, listening to himself asking the question of who was inside the room with him when he heard the disembodied female voice. After hearing himself ask the question, he caught a distant voice inside the audio. After enhancing it, he played the audio once again and caught the voice.

"Is that who I think it was." Donovan said.

"Bridget Bishop was in the home with us."

Vail and Donovan later appeared at a City Hall meeting in Salem with the city council and residents of the city. Vail and Donovan showed the audience all the information and evidence that they discovered inside the witch house. The audience was sort of stunned by the evidence. The last evidence that was shown was the voice of Bridget Bishop. Upon playing the audio for the audience and council, they were quietly appalled. Afterwards the gave applause to Vail and Donovan. Thanking them for their visit and their investigation.

Upon leaving Salem the following day, Donovan asked Vail what his next investigation would be if he already knew. Vail, sitting inside his car turned and faced Donovan. He gave a small smirk.

"From what I can guess, my next case will probably be out of the ordinary."

THE FOG FROM WITHIN

49

Many areas across the middle of The United States have reported sightings of a strange Fog that arrives in their cities and towns and causing a great disturbance throughout neighborhoods and counties. Many reports speak of strange anomalies inside the Fog itself. Some resemble human beings, others see animals, or other types of strange things that basically live inside The Fog.

Travis Vail has now been contacted by many of the cities and towns to investigate the mysterious Fog. As Vail prepares himself to investigate the sightings, he begins to think to himself what he can back up on the mysterious Fog. The first city that Vail investigates is Boulder, Colorado. As Vail enters Boulder, he meets with a few of the residents that reside in Boulder that reported The Fog's appearance.

While speaking with the residents and listening to their view of The Fog's appearance for over several hours, Vail noticed many of the residents had particularly seen the anomalies moving inside The Fog. Upon further research about the mysterious Fog, Vail discovers that the Fog was seen centuries ago after the genocide of many soldiers and innocent people.

Vail contacted his fellow Historian, Raynard Brown to investigate the history of the mysterious Fog. Raynard suggests that the Fog was created by way of witchcraft, possibly due to Pagan rituals and celebrations. Vail takes those suggestions into his mind and keeps them there for further references later throughout his investigations. Vail continued to speak with many other residents who've seen the Fog in front of their homes. Vail declares to Boulder's Mayor that he will begin an investigation throughout the neighborhood that night, which the Mayor allowed with no problems.

The following night, Vail walked throughout the neighborhood, awaiting the possible appearance of The Fog. He doesn't feel anything unusual nor see anything that resembles paranormal. Though, Vail noticed the wind began to pick up slowly as the trees slowly moved along with the cold breeze. Vail walked through the empty streets in the neighborhood, following the breeze's whereabouts. As he walked closer to the breeze, he hears a sudden whistle. Vail turned and seen no one behind him.

"If anyone is out here, please state your name and purpose."

No individual makes themselves known before Vail as he continued to walk down the street. He continued to follow the breeze.

The following day, Vail continued to study on the Fog

and its ghostly inhabitants. Raynard contacts him once again and they discuss the Fog and its possibilities of being conjured by a Pagan cult through Witchcraft or a possible supernatural entity that only appears during the Winter season of the year. Vail continued to take those suggestions to his mind and began focusing on the Pagan root of the Fog. Vail later set a return date to Boulder after he visit's the other cities that have been reporting The Fog.

Vail arrived in Topeka, Kansas, where The Fog had reportedly attacked individuals in the streets during a Christmas festival event. Vail speaks with Topeka's Mayor and the residents who were present during the Christmas festival. Upon listening to the residents and even the Mayor's own account of The Fog, Vail tells the Mayor that he will have an investigation of the location later that night. The Mayor allowed him to have his investigation and commanded police to close the whole area just for Vail to have complete clearance to proceed with his investigation.

Later that night, police gather around the entire area of where The Fog attacked the festival. Vail walked throughout the area, seeing its damaged Christmas lights and stands on the ground. Vail began to call out The Fog by yelling out names of Pagan gods and goddesses. Though, Vail had seen no signs of The Fog or anything that was related to Paganism or the paranormal.

The next day, Vail thanked the Mayor for his time in Topeka, yet having not seen The Fog himself, Vail continued his investigations across the other cities. Vail decides to head over to Tulsa, Oklahoma to discuss The Fog's appearance within their city. Upon entering Tulsa,

Vail is highly greeted by the residents of Tulsa and their
Mayor. Vail talked with all of them during an assembly as
the residents each stood up and took their chance at telling
Vail what they seen about The Fog.

Vail investigated Tulsa that night and begins to feel
something unusual in the air. He looked around himself
and turned toward the streets in front of him. Vail sees
what looked to be three anomalies approaching him. As
Vail decided to walk toward the anomalies, he sees a giant
white mist behind them, which he cannot see through.

"There's the Fog." Vail said.

Vail stared at The Fog as it approached him. Through
its path it knocked down street signs, destroyed windows on
buildings and nearby cars and even made the ground itself
tremble as if a miniature earthquake erupted in Tulsa. Vail
did not run from The Fog as it approached him even closer.
Vail stood his ground as The Fog ran right through him. As
Vail was inside The Fog, he seen many spirits walking
through The Fog. Vail quickly stared and studied the spirits
that walked past him, noticing their outfits resemble the
mid-1800s. Vail sees soldiers that appeared to have died
during the Civil War and even sees innocent civilians
walking through The Fog. Inside the Fog feels like a giant
fan is blowing directly in front of you. Vail continued to
stand his ground as the wind began to pick up as The Fog
was coming to an end.

While the Fog was coming to its end, Vail noticed six
druids walking slowly at the end of The Fog. Wearing black
and red cloak with their hoods on. They were silent and
didn't even glance at Vail as they walked right past him.
Vail turned and watched the druids leave as The Fog ended.
The druids and spirits disappeared in the air along with The

Fog.

"That was something I've never encountered."

The next day, Vail told Tulsa's Mayor about The Fog and said that he has no idea what could conjure it up, though it may have already been finished. Afterwards, Vail returned to Topeka, where he tells the Mayor and residents that he seen The Fog back in Tulsa and said that it might not return. Vail last returned to Boulder, where he has a conversation with the Mayor. After their conversation, Vail began to leave Boulder as the Mayor approached him.

"It's a good thing that you came in time before Christmas." The Mayor said.

"Hope the residents are happy with their Christmas."

"Do you celebrate Christmas, Mr. Vail? It's just a question because you seem like a man who doesn't have time for holidays."

"I celebrate certain days. Not Christmas."

"Why is that?"

"I'm not Pagan."

Vail walked away, getting into his car, driving away.

THE REVENANCY VOYAGE

The ship that's known as *The Revenancy* was one of the most graceful and respected ships that has ever sailed across the Atlantic Ocean. Its service ran for over three decades until its untimely demise after it was attacked and raided by pirates of the European Union. Now, the ship sits on a dock near the Atlantic Ocean where it is presented as a historical relic and used for tourism.

The ship is also known for its large amount of haunting after its demise. Many people who have went into the ship have reported paranormal disturbances throughout the entire ship. Some have reported footsteps, voices, moans, and even screams. One reported that a lamp was thrown toward them. Due to the increase of reports, the current owner of the ship has contacted Travis Vail to investigate the ship's haunting.

Within a few days, Vail arrived in Charleston, North Carolina to the dock where the ship is currently residing. Along with Vail is Colton Levi, his longtime assistance in the paranormal. They approach the owner of the ship, Clay Haskett. He approaches them as they greet each other.

Haskett allows them into his office.

"It's a great honor to finally meet you, Mr. Vail."

"No worries, Mr. Haskett." Vail said. "So, what have you with these reports of the ship?"

"We've received many, if not dozens more of reports that contain paranormal incidents within the ship."

"What kind of incidents, if I may ask." Colton said.

"Voices, footsteps, moans and groans." Haskett said. "One report contained a lamp being thrown."

"Seems to me that these are spirits that do not want to be disturbed or have a darker history that what we were told by the officials." Vail said.

"What's your current plan, Mr. Vail?"

"Colton and I will walk through the ship and I will head over to your museum to do more research on the ship's history."

Haskett stood up from his desk and walked towards the door. He opened it and stood by, allowing Vail and Colton to approach the ship.

"May we enter the ship?" Vail said.

"Of course." Haskett said. "Just don't try to startle the tourists, please."

"Sure. No problem."

Vail and Colton enter the ship. Passing by tourists who are laughing and taking photos with each other.

"Try not to get distracted, Colton."

"No worries."

They entered the lounge area of the ship, noticing many tourists inside taking photos. Colton tells Vail to search another area of the ship before the lounge, due to the number of tourists within the lounge. Vail agrees with Colton as they approach the other rooms of the ship. After a left turn down a hall, they notice rooms that appear to be hotel rooms.

"This was used as a hotel facility?" Colton said.

"Appears to be so." Vail said. "This is new to me and I wonder what else will present itself."

They scanned the hotel rooms, searching for evidence. Upon approaching the other rooms, Colton heard a distant moan from deeper within the hall. Vail looked up and down the hall, seeing no one in sight.

"You heard it too." Colton said.

"I did." Vail said. "I suggest we take a look before we head out."

Vail and Colton walk down the hall, taking slow and quick looks in the rooms nearby searching for whatever the moan came from. They reach the end of the hall and find nothing that relates to the moan. Vail turned to Colton, suggesting they head to the museum for further research. As they walk back down the hall, a book is thrown at the wall in front of Vail. He stops walking and turns to his left, looking in a room where the book flew from.

"It seems these spirits are not too friendly." Vail said. "We better get moving and we'll return later tonight for our investigation."

They exit out the ship, seeing Haskett approaching them nervously.

"Did you find anything as of this moment?"

"There's something inside this ship and we'll find it tonight when we return." Vail said. "Nothing to worry about, Mr. Haskett. We will solve the problem."

Vail and Colton leave the dock of *The Revenancy* as Haskett looks at the ship with a little sign of fear.

At the Charleston Museum, Vail and Colton gather books containing historical records of *The Revenancy* and its historical tragic voyage. After reading through a few books and scanning their notes, Vail realizes that the ship was used in a cruise line and even in military use. He even finds a record that contains information of the crew being murdered by pirates near the European Union.

"This ship has some very dark history." Vail said. "Being used for military warfare as well as a cruise ship."

"What shall we focus on during the investigation tonight?" Colton said.

"We'll focus on the spirits that reside in the ship." Vail said. "Try to find a way for them to cross over."

Vail closed the books, placing them on their shelves before leaving the museum.

Near nightfall, they return to the ship where Haskett waits for them. He sees them and approaches them.

"You two sure you're ready for this?"

"We've done far much worse than this, Mr. Haskett." Vail said. "There won't be any problems tonight.:

Vail and Colton enter *The Revenancy* as Haskett leaves the dock. Once inside the ship, the silence air slowly brings up a chill to Colton.

"It's deeply quiet in here."

"Don't run off on this one, Colton." Vail said. "You've been inside a prison where hell basically took place. Don't let a ship scare you near death."

They approached the lounge. Now, it's not crowded by the tourists from earlier in the day. Vail looked around the lounge for any clues. Colton searches the other side of the lounge.

"See anything?" Vail said.

"Nothing yet." Colton said. "Sure, something will make itself present."

"It will make itself present." Vail said. "Maybe sooner than we're expecting it to present."

While searching the lounge, they hear a distant yell coming from the dwells of the ship. Colton turned to Vail, who tells him to walk down the hall near the yell's whereabouts. Colton slowly walked down the hall, somewhat a little startled.

"Is anyone here with me?" Colton said. "I'm just asking to be a little perspective."

A bucket had suddenly fell from a shelf in front of Colton. He stopped and looked at the bucket. Vail walked behind him and approached the bucket.

"You're not afraid of a water bucket, are you?" Vail asked. "Because it seemed to startle you."

"I'm doing just fine, Vail." Colton said. "No problems at all."

Vail continued to walk down the hall, passing by rooms that resembled a dining hall where many of the passenger had dinner and occasional parties. Colton looked in the room seeing the tables and banners which were inside the ship. Through a few turns down the right hall, Vail discovers a room that is packed with medical equipment.

"This must be the medical room." Vail said. "It's highly possible that many people died inside this room."

"It's sure able to have a pack of spiritual energy in here." Colton said.

"The energy is here, Colton, and it's getting stronger as we're in here."

Vail looked around the room. He told Colton to take

out the digital recorder and place it on the table. Vail stood by the recorder on the table.

"I am Travis Vail, and this is Colton Levi. We are here to speak with any spirits who reside in this *Revenancy* ship. We're here to discover your existence and to send you over into the afterlife."

A sound creaked from the medical room's door. Colton turned and stared as Vail continued to talk by the digital recorder.

"Vail, looks like something is in here with us."

"I hear it Colton. Whoever has entered this room, please speak into this recorder device on this table next to me to respond to my questions."

Colton stood by the door, looking out down the hall as Vail began asking questions toward the spirits. Vail asked if the spirits worked on the ship during its military run or its cruise line run. They caught a voice that said military, which Vail believes it's a military Navy officer that must have died on the ship in the line of duty. Colton looked further down the hall and saw what appeared to be a silhouette of a man wearing a casual Ship Captain uniform walking into the dining room.

"Vail, I just saw an apparition down the hall. It walked into the dining room."

"I suggest you go and look. If you, please."

Colton walked down the hall and entered the dining room. Seeing no one inside the room, he turned back to the exit. Once he turned, he was staring a Ship Captain right in the eyes. Colton yelled and ran back towards the medical room. Vail paused and ran out of the room towards Colton.

"What's wrong?" Vail asked.

"It was standing in my face!" Colton said. "Right in my

face!"

"What did you see?"

"I saw the ship captain staring me right in the eyes. A complete stare. I thought it lasted for eternity, yet it was a few seconds."

Vail looked out the window and saw the sun beginning to rise, signaling the end of their investigation. He turned toward Colton and looked down the hall.

"Seems our investigation is done." Vail said.

Vail grabbed the recorder as they left the ship.

The following day, Vail speaks with Haskett about the investigation and tells him about the Navy soldier that spoke about the military as well as Colton's sighting of the ship's captain. Vail says the spirits have claimed the ship their home. Haskett thanked Vail and Colton for their service. They leave the dock and Colton turned to Vail.

"This ship freaked me our more than the prison we've once visited."

"*The Revenancy* will continue to scare people towards the point of death."

"May I ask what's next on the horizon of the paranormal?"

"Whatever comes my way."

THE FOREST OF THE VANISHING

61

Within the outskirts of Seattle, Washington is a mysterious forest that many decide not to enter due to its intensive history of people vanishing without a trace. Animals walk through the area calmly and are not disturb. Only human beings are the ones that walk through with fear and paranoia who are later vanished. News reports have scattered across the nation with concerns of the forest being burned down to avoid any more people going missing. The debate is currently ongoing amongst the Washington State Governor and the US Government.

The occult detective known as Travis Vail arrived in Seattle as he prepared to do an investigation by himself inside the forest. While walking through downtown Seattle, Vail decided to meet with Seattle's Mayor to discuss his investigation into the forest. As Vail walked down the streets, he spotted the Mayor delivering a speech outside in the open with over a dozen residents standing and listening. Vail stood in the back of the crowd as he watched the Mayor talk about their city's future.

After the mayor finished his speech and the residents

began to leave the area, Vail approached the Mayor. As he introduced himself, the Mayor instantly recognized who Vail was and they entered a small office inside a nearby building. While inside the office, Vail discussed to the Mayor of investigating the Vanishing Forest. After about an hour through the conversation, the Mayor gives Vail his blessing and Vail leaves the office building, heading towards the forest itself.

Vail entered the outskirts of Seattle and stands not too far from the highway. He began walking toward the tree and noticed a medium-sized sign sitting on his left side of the field, saying *"Do Not Enter! Forbidden Area."*. Vail smirked and started walking into the forest. As he proceeded through the quiet and smelly forest, he noticed ahead of him was a small shrine. As Vail inched closer to the shrine, he spotted it was built upon with bones of what appeared to be a buffalo.

"What is this." Vail said.

Vail began to step into the middle of the shrine, though being cautious. As Vail turned around, looking at the surrounds, he realized that there was more than one shrine. There was a total of thirteen shrines. The shrines were decorated with crosses, candles, bones, skulls of various animals and some even human, meaning there were possible animal and human sacrifices within the forest at some point. As Vail approaches each of the shrines, he knows that this is a site of a pagan ritual and burial ground. To his mind, he sees that as being a possible reason why many people have disappeared while inside the forest. Vail also spotted a few obelisks standing inside the forest as well that stood near twelve feet in height.

"Why would they choose a place such as this?" Vail

said.

Vail continued to examine the surrounding shrines within the forest. As he studied each shrine and what it was built upon. While he was aware of the location of which he was standing in, he began to move very slowly. The forest began to grow a fog in the air, surrounding the shrines that Vail was studying. He began to write down every shrine that stood in the forest and the description of the shrines. While writing, Vail heard a distant sound coming from his left inside the forest. He stopped writing and walked over to the noise. Hearing a slowly dripping sound, he walked near the noise. Going through the fog that's growing larger and thicker. Vail stopped and looked down as he saw what appeared to be blood dripping from a tree nearby. As Vail looked up toward the tree, he finds an array of decorated skulls sitting and hanging on the tree.

"What did they do in this place?"

Vail backed away from the tree and decided to continue writing down the other shrines before leaving. As he wrote down the last shrine, he felt the wind blowing behind his neck, he turned as it began to pick up with the fog slowly evaporating into the air. Vail noticed that something was going on inside the forest. As The wind continued to blow, Vail spotted what appeared to be shoes laying on the ground. He ran over toward them and picked one up. Upon looking at it, the shoe belonged to a young boy. Vail looked around the spot for any other trace. Only finding the two shoes, he took them with him as he decided to leave the forest. As Vail walked through the forest, finding his way back. He begins to feel nauseous and drained. He placed his hand on his head, shaking it so he can focus.

"I don't know what you are. Now leave me be."

Vail regained his focus as he left the forest and returned to Seattle to show the Mayor the shoes and the shrines inside the forest.

Later that afternoon, Vail spoke with the Mayor about the shoes and the shrines that laid inside the forest. The Mayor began to call on a police force to head into the forest to search for the missing boy. Vail declined the force as the Mayor was running out of ideas as of who to send inside the forest. Vail looked at the Mayor and stated that he was returning to the forest that night to do a full complete investigation of the forest and the shrines. Believing that something might be going on during the night rather than the day. The Mayor paused as he returned to his desk and nodded. Giving Vail his answer to go into the forest after dawn. Vail left the Mayor's Office and headed toward Seattle's Museum of History and Industry to study more on the forest and its disappeared victims.

As the sun began to set and many of Seattle's residents were awaiting Vail's word of entering the forest, Vail approached the forest from the same direction as before, only this time, Vail carried a bottle of holy water and even his ritual book as he entered, which would only mean that something more was going on inside the forest with the shrines. Vail nodded to himself as he returned into the forest. Now, walking through the forest in pitch darkness and only hearing the echoes of animals, insects, and the sticks and branches breaking and cracking underneath his feet as he walked, Vail focused on the shrines and the feeling of being drained earlier before he left.

A distant flutter approached Vail from his right side. He quickly turned, looking through the darkness of the forest. Not seeing anything unusual, he continued walking through. Knowing he felt uneasy inside the forest, he continued walking as he approached the area of the shrines. Vail stood in the middle of the location, where all the shrines were facing. He rubbed some of the holy water on his forehead and held his ritual book close to his heart.

"I know you're here. I know you're all here."

Vail held his arms out as he turned around, making a full circle, while holding the book in his hand.

"Whatever you are. Whatever you've done to these people. I declare that you stop your terrorizing and return to the other side where you belong."

Not seeing or hearing anything, Vail continued to call out whatever was lurking inside the forest, which is responsible for the dozens of disappearances throughout the years. As Vail continued, he felt that something was watching him inside the forest. He stopped talking and looked around.

"I can feel you watching me. So, why don't you come on out, so I can see you."

Vail stood still as the wind picked up once again. Vail could smell the evaporation inside the forest. As he looked around, he began to hear moans coming from each of the shrines. He looked at them as he seen druids from all over approach him. Vail noticed that the druids are all in different pairs, each pair is arriving from one shrine. Each pair was covered with six druids. Vail stared at the pairs as he realized it was seventy-eight druids that were approaching him. The druids slowly surrounded him in a circle with the leaders of the pairs approaching Vail inside the circle. The druids wore all black cloaks with hoods covering their faces.

"I demand that you tell me who you are and who you worship." Vail said.

The druids stopped and only faced Vail. None of the druids speak or make any sudden noises as Vail stared at them.

"I suggest you say something about the missing people."

The druids stood silently as Vail walked around them. He glanced at the druids that circled him as well as the leading druids. As Vail walked around, he glanced toward one of the druids that stood on the outside. Looking at its height and size, Vail realized that druid had to be a child. He ran over toward the druid as the others approaching him and shoved him back into the circle. Vail looked at the leading druids and glanced back at the child druid.

"Who is that child? Answer me! Who's the child?!"

One of the leading druids approached Vail and raised his head, facing Vail. Vail stood his ground as he took an extra step toward the druid.

"I will ask again. Who's the child druid?"

"The druid you speak of is the child that the common people consider a missing person."

"You're saying to me that the child is the one that I'm looking for?"

"Indeed. That child is one of us now."

Vail rubbed his head as he looked at the other druids that surrounded him. He turned back to the leading druid as he pointed out the surrounding druids.

"So, who are the other druids circling me? Are they the other missing or vanished people?"

"Yes. They are the vanished ones. They came into our forest, stepped onto our sacred land and decided to disobey the oath that stood on this land for centuries."

"You can't keep these people here. They need to return to their homes and families."

"Their families wouldn't accept them the way they are today. They have changed greatly and with a cost they can't turn away from."

"What are you saying exactly?"

"The people you see around you on this day are not the same people that vanished throughout the centuries. If they were to return to their previous grounds, they would only destroy not only the ones they loved and cared for, but also the land they lived upon."

Vail nodded as he raised his book and held it in the face of the druid.

"I'm sending you and these people back."

"If you know the words of which to say."

"I do."

Vail began reading from the book as the wind picked up again. The druids began to back away from Vail as he continued reading. The surrounding druids had disappeared and only the leading druids remained. Vail continued as each druid disappeared one at a time. As he read from the book, the druid he was speaking withstood still and watched Vail read from the book. Vail looked up toward the druid with energy flowing through him.

"Time for you to go."

"I will leave this time. But, listen carefully Mr. Vail, there will come the time that I shall not leave, and neither will you."

The druid slowly backed away and disappeared through the wind. The wind had stopped as Vail finished reading from the book. He exhales as he placed the book back into his coat pocket and proceeded to leave the forest.

The following day, Vail spoke with the Mayor and the residents of Seattle about the forest and what he had seen the previous night. Mainly frightening the residents, he told them about the druids and how they were all the people who reportedly went missing or vanished without a trace. Vail said they were in a better place and that no one should ever enter the forest again. The residents applauded Vail for his bravery as he and the Mayor left the stage. The Mayor thanked him for visiting Seattle and hoped he would return. Vail turned and nodded.

"I will make my return when the time is accurate to do so."

Vail entered his black 1970 impala and drove down the highway, leaving the city of Seattle.

THE ABANDONED HOTEL

During the early fall season and with heavy snowfall, Travis Vail traveled past Vancouver, Canada, heading towards an abandoned hotel named The Black Raven. The hotel is known for its prestigious setting as well as its number of floors. The floors of the hotel are a total of thirteen floors and all of them have a large majority of haunting that witnesses have suspected to be spiritual and demonic occurrences, some have even been attacked by the unseen forces.

Vail arrived at the Black Raven Hotel and found no one there but himself. While walking closer to the front entrance of the abandoned hotel, he heard a vehicle approaching him from behind. He took a turn around to see the vehicle and its driver. The vehicle parked next to his and the driver exited.

"I do not know who you are or where you come from, but you cannot enter this place." The driver said.

"Why shouldn't I enter?" Vail said. "Is it because of the spirits?"

"Yes sir. I'm giving you a fair warning here. I heard that some guy was going to go inside the place and try to contact those things in there. You make a mistake. You could release them out here."

"Judging by the way you speak, you do not understand the spiritual realm nor its duties." Vail said. "You are speaking with the Spirit-Seeker and there aren't many as I in this field. So, please do me a favor and return to your home in peace and leave the spirits to me."

Vail turned away from the driver and approached the hotel entrance doors. The driver, filled with emotions, ran over toward Vail and snatched him by his right arm, trying to pull him away from the doors.

"You need to leave this place, sir!" The driver said. "It is not safe to be here at this particular time and season!"

"Unhand me or I will suggest placing you inside this hotel and you can deal with those who are unseen to the human eyes."

"You wouldn't do that to me. I'm just an ordinary guy. I have a job, I have a wife, children, a home, a car. I have a life. I'm just trying to get you to understand that you must save yours before you make a mistake."

Vail stared at the driver and smiled.

"As always. Men like you aren't truly built for what awaits you after this life you're currently living in. Men like you will never fully awaken to understand what lies behind the scales that cover your sight. You and people like you are blinded to the truth and you never seek to find it nor the ones who hide it. Therefore, you are wasting your time trying to change my ways because I've already chosen my path as it presented itself before me."

"You must not enter this place! You cannot! Its suicide!"

"Suicide is what you do when you've given up your belief and strength in things beyond your comprehension."

Vail snatched his arm back from the driver and approached the hotel doors. He placed his hand on the door handles and pulled them back toward him. The hotel doors swung open as if a gust of wind had blown out of the hotel and into the open area. The driver panicked and ran to his car, screaming for his life.

"You've opened the doors! You've released the spirits!"

The driver pulled back and drove away as Vail watched him leave and gave a slight smirk.

"Now, let us see who's waiting for me in here."

Vail walked into the hotel and looked at its interior lobby area. Vail took a few more steps into the lobby area, the two entrance doors shut as if someone had closed them from the inside. Vail looked back and circled the lobby.

"I fully understand that there are thirteen floors in this place and I intend to search them all before the night is fully over. I hope those of you in this place can and will understand that."

Vail walked by an elevator, knowing there was no electricity operating inside the hotel since its abandonment. Vail walked past the elevator and as he approached the end of the hallway toward the staircase, a small bell rang behind him. Vail turned back and sees the elevator light blinking.

"Interesting and intriguing."

Vail walked back toward the elevator and the doors opened as if it was set up for him to enter. Vail nodded and entered the elevator. The door shut and the elevator operations as if it was still in use. The elevator goes up and stopped at the second floor, the door opened, and Vail exited the elevator.

"I take it that someone is on my side in this place."

Vail found himself in the hallway of the second floor and all that surrounded him are the rooms and the equipment which was left behind before its closing. He walked through most of the hotel searching for any signs of spirits. Not finding anything related to the spirits in the rooms on the second floor, Vail went toward the staircase door and the elevator dinged again. Vail turned toward the elevator and its door opened once more. Vail chuckled as he entered.

"Third floor I take it."

The elevator moved up and stopped. Its door opened, allowing Vail to step onto the third floor of the hotel. Vail stepped out and felt a gust of wind move past him. Vail quickly turned to his right and saw a shroud of mist hovering through the hallway, entering a room without the door being opened.

"Here we go."

Vail ran toward the room door and opened it. He gazed around and doesn't spot the mist which flew into the room, although he can hear what appeared to be people talking amongst themselves in the hallway, which doesn't startle him, but raised his awareness of his surroundings.

"There's more of you on this floor I take it. Proves very interesting."

Vail stepped out into the hallway and could still hear the voices speaking to each other as if they were having a conversation to themselves. Vail reached into his coat pocket and pulled out the book of rituals. He raised the book up above his head and circled in his steps.

"You see this book I hold above me, spirits? This book will send you into the Other Side, where you all will be judged for your actions here on earth and will prove your eternal place."

A form of wind began to pick up from inside the hallway, Vail continued to speak toward the voices and held the book above his head. Vail continued as he saw shady forms of humans, all appeared to be yelling at him in anger and hatred. Vail knew these kinds of spirits and raised his voice as he spoke to them.

"I will not repeat myself to you spirits of the demonic darkness!" Vail said loudly. "You will respond to me and you will enter the Other Side and be judged for your earthly account."

The spirits screamed toward Vail as each of them began to fly toward him and entered the wall behind him. Vail never flinched when the spirits flew pass him. He continued to speak to them and held the book continuously above his head.

Vail understood a few of the spirits had indeed went over to the Other Side while the remaining ones had decided to remain in the hotel to attack Vail in any shape they could.

"I know you've traveled to the upper levels of this hotel, spirits. I intend greatly to seek you out and to release you from this place you currently call your home."

Vail walked toward the elevator and it no longer worked. Vail shrugged his shoulders, taking the stairs up to the fourth floor. Upon arriving on the fourth floor, Vail didn't receive any communication or sound from a spirit of any kind. He searched every room on the floor to make sure there wasn't a spirit hiding amongst his presence.

"Fourth floor appears to be clean." Vail said as he checked the last room.

He went up into the fifth floor and all he could see around him was trash and left-over furniture sitting out in the hallway. The hallway had an odor resembling a dumpster, which would be sitting out back or on the side of the hotel, though there were no dumpsters near the hotel. Vail searched every room on the fifth floor, jumping over rugged and molded furniture to get into some rooms. Some of the rooms had a damp feeling and they possessed the smell of damp air after a rainfall.

"Fifth floor is clean. Spiritually clean I might add."

Vail arrived on the sixth floor and as soon as he took a step forward, a mist of cold air blew past him. He could feel the presence of a spirit, whether it be human or demonic. Vail smirked as he walked slowly down the hallway, which was much cleaner than the fifth floor.

"Finally, one of you has started to present yourself toward me and of all the floors you decide to pick the sixth floor. Guess six is your lucky number."

"We do not like your trespassing, hunter." A disembodied voice said from the hallway.

"I heard that very clearly and I would like for you to speak to me again, so I can get a sense of your character and afterwards send you to the Other Side." Vail said.

"We demand you leave our home." The disembodied voice commanded.

"I'm not leaving this hotel until all of you are gone from it and it becomes nothing more than an old building waiting to be crumbled down."

A loud scream shrieked through the hallway, Vail covered his ears quickly to avoid minor damage to his ears. The shriek had immediately stopped. Vail removed his hands from his ears and the entire hallway was dead silent.

"Whatever you are and where ever you've come from, I am here to send you to another place where you will never escape your fate."

After searching the entire sixth floor, Vail continued to make his way upward toward the remaining floors, seven through thirteen. On the seventh floor, during Vail's searching of the rooms, he found a note which was left behind by someone who was either staying or working in the hotel. Vail read the note as it had implied there was some otherworldly force that dwelled before he hotel closed. Vail placed the note in his coat pocket.

"Seems you've been here a while." Vail said.

The eighth floor possessed neither anything related to the supernatural nor were any spirits contacted by Vail throughout the entire floor. The ninth floor possessed very little furniture and a shortage of rooms, whereas the first eight floors were settled with a total of twenty rooms where the ninth floor had a total of ten rooms. Vail kept his patience in check as he noticed there were no spirits being found within the upper floors.

"I know you're here and you are waiting on me to find you, yes?" Vail said. "I will find you and we will have our confrontation."

Vail stepped foot onto the tenth floor and spotted a difference in the air. A change of sorts which could only be caused by a weather effect, though it was continuing to snow on the outside, whereas the interior of the tenth floor felt a mixture of cold and heat. Vail had placed into his mind that he was dealing with a spirit or spirits that were unlike any he has encountered in his previous investigations.

"If you are on this floor with me, make yourselves known unto me." Vail said. "I heard one of you speak to me on the sixth floor and I demand that you speak to me now before I reach the thirteen floor and end this for good."

"Why have you come here, Travis Vail, the Spirit-Seeker." A voice said from the other end of the hallway. "You seem to be determined to eliminate us from our dwelling place and yet here we are."

Vail couldn't see the figure from the other end due to a dark mist covering its presence. Vail pulled out a flare and threw it toward the middle of the hallway. The flare lit up most of the hallway and all Vail could gather by his sight was a figure and on its hands were long sharpened nails and its eyes were like the cold sky to him.

"Come. Come Travis Vail. Follow me up to the thirteen-floor and you will receive what you've come for." The voice said as it disappeared.

Vail ran toward the other end of the hall, fanning away the dark mist that covered the end. Vail saw nothing and ran up toward the thirteen-floor, surpassing the eleventh and twelfth floors. Vail ran unto he reached the door that would lead him to the thirteen-floor. Vail kicked the door opened and looked around, realizing that the floor was a place where people would stay. The thirteen-floor appeared to be an office of some kind, apparently a secret office.

"What kind of place is this?" Vail questioned.

"This is our dwelling place, Spirit-Seeker." The voice said. "As is mine."

The voice appeared closer toward Vail as the entity revealed itself to him. The entity appeared to be a hybrid of both man and demon. Vail took a step back as he stared at the creature, never seeing a living being of that kind before in his lifetime.

"What in the hell are you?"

"I am known throughout the ages as Kamagrauto, servant of Dagor, the Soul Eater."

"Dagor? Soul Eater? What in the hell are you speaking about, demon beast?!"

"It seems you've never studied in the occult as deep as you thought. We're always hearing about what your work has done for many in the world. From your little stop at a mansion to that forest of druids. We know of you, Spirit-Seeker."

Vail stared at Kamagrauto, scanning the room for any others that might appear before him on the thirteen-floor.

"How have you been watching me? Why have you been watching me and for what purpose?"

"You are one of our enemies, Travis Vail." Kamagrauto said. "You and countless others all share the same goal of eliminating our kind from this earth to leave only the righteous alive to subdue it."

"There aren't others like me, demon. If there were, I would've already made myself known to them."

"The intriguing part of this meeting here is all of you mostly have encountered one another in the past at some point in time. Whether it was a small crossover or a passing by on the road. You've all met at some point in time and you all will meet each other again in the coming future, but that will be the moment where all of you get agree to join sides to face us."

"This isn't making any sense. I'm about to send you over."

Vail pulled out his book and raised it over his head. Kamagrauto laughed at Vail for doing the task. He even started clapping his hands and rubbing his sharp nails together to sidetrack Vail's focus.

"That little book isn't going to work on me, Vail. I am beyond an ordinary spirit. I was created by my master Dagor and only through him may I be put away."

"I won't let you leave this place alive and intact, demon." Vail said. "You must leave this place and take the remaining spirits with you."

"Why do you think I'm here?" Kamagrauto said. "I'm here on orders from Dagor to collect as many souls as possible and bring them back to him for observation."

"What is he observing them for?"

"Why to consume them of course and go gain as much strength as he needs to succeed in his plans."

"I will not allow such destruction to be cause in my presence!" Vail said as he ran toward Kamagrauto.

"You small pest."

Kamagrauto lifted Vail up off the ground and threw him against the wall as a frame that was hanging on the wall fell onto his head, cutting his forehead open.

"Very well, I will be leaving now, Travis Vail and we will indeed come across paths once again. But, that day will most certainly be your final investigation."

Kamagrauto vanished in a puff of smoke as Vail ran

after it. Seeing nothing but an empty room, Vail leaves the thirteen floor and travels back down to the first floor. The sun began to shine down on Vail as he walked outside and sealed the hotel doors shut. He entered his car and drove away. Though, in his mind was Kamagrauto's words of what would come concerning Dagor and others whose work was similar to Vail's own.

TRAVIS VAIL, SPIRIT-SEEKER: FIRST SINS

I

<u>WHAT CAME BEFORE</u>

Reading through his past investigations and encounters with the otherworldly, Travis Vail, known in the occult circles as the Spirit-Seeker, is researching more of his past encounter with Kamagrauto, the demon who opened his mind to the larger world. After the visitation from Kamagrauto at the Black Raven Hotel and in finding the Mutant-Thing, Vail is curious about the world he's about to enter. A world where the supernatural comes into conflict with the rising heroes. A mixture that will only end in chaos.

Still studying, Vail's phone rang, and he answered with slight haste and ease of movement. His instincts were still kicking. His mind on Kamagrauto's words and his encounter with Abraham and The Swordman.

"Vail speaking."

"Trav, good to hear your voice."

"Ah. Dr. Galen Donovan." Vail said with a smirk. "Same here. Why have you called?"

"I have a case for you. If you're interested."

"What kind of case if I may ask humbly?"

"From what I've learned, it concerns the first sins?"

"First sins? As in the first sins committed after the Fall?"

"Correct."

Vail nodded. "I'm on board. Send me the details and I'll follow suit."

"Will do." Donovan said. "You'll have the information shortly."

Vail hung up and within several minutes, the information was sent to Vail through his email. Reading the files, Vail learned the first sins were moving through the world in slow form. Unusual to his previous encounters in past cases, there was a map attached to the files which detailed the past locations of the sins' movements. Vail packed his gear, what was needed, grabbed his black trench coat and left his lair.

Following the map's layout, Vail went across most of the United Kingdom into France and into Germany. Vail has spoken with several witnesses to the sightings and they explained the sins appeared as one. Embodied to moving around single filed. Whatever it was, it had no motives other than to terrorize and to instill fear into the humans it came across. After each movement it made, the more aggressive it became. From startling humans to torturing them if came close.

"This is something else." Vail noted. "Something far more powerful is at work here than just some series of haunting."

Vail continued his investigations and interviews for the next several days. During those days, Vail began to come across what looked to be plague doctors. Crouched in the shadows to walking past him in crowds. Vail took nothing from it until he managed to see one staring at him from the distance. The plague doctor dressed in an all-black robe. Covered from head to toe with its doctor's mask sticking out of its hood. Vail smirked.

"You think that frightens me, lad? Tell you what, take off that beak and we'll settle this like men."

The plague doctor stood still. Vail waited, yet, nothing came from the doctor.

"Figures." Vail said. "I'm going on about my business. Don't try to follow or you'll end up somewhere you won't like."

Vail contacted Donovan concerning the case and the uprising of plague doctors. Donovan stated the doctors are probably the result of the sins' travels. The doctors are following the path of the sins.

"They may be, but, there's something more to all of

this. Something sinister at work."

"Why don't we meet up and discuss our ideas on this case?"

"Sure. Where are you right now?"

"In Italy."

"Let me guess, Venice."

"I'm having a word with Ms. Belinda Grazio. You remember her I presume?"

"I can't forget a face like hers. Anyhow, I'm leaving Germany. I'll be there as fast as possible."

"Take your time. Belinda is patient of your coming."

"She would be."

II

<u>WHAT CAME AFTER</u>

Vail entered the city of Venice near nightfall. Vail had walked through Venice reaching the hotel. When Vail came closer, he could see Donovan standing outside of a door.

"There he is." Vail said walking.

Vail made his way toward Donovan and the two hugged.

"You came quicker than I expected."

"I was on the move right after our conversation."

"Good timing."

"Not my best, but I try."

Vail investigated the hotel room. He saw no one inside. He gazed his eyes toward Donovan while pointing into the room. Donovan looked back into the room and turned to Vail.

"Looking for something?"

"I thought you said Belinda was here?"

"She's at her home." Donovan said. "She will meet with

us in the morning. In the meantime, you and I need to discuss this case."

"Sure thing."

Vail entered the hotel room and Donovan followed. Inside, they sat at the coffee table. Atop the table were files Donovan had brought with him. The same documents he emailed to Vail to begin with. Donovan had passed Vail a bottle of beer and Vail drank.

"Plague doctors?" Donovan asked with confusion.

"I saw them at every location the sins had come across. They just stood there. Staring. I taunted one."

"Sounds like something you'll do."

"What would you do if you had a plague doctor staring down at you from across the area?"

"Where did the doctor go?"

"Not sure. I walked away afterwards. Warned it if it followed me it would end up in a far worse place."

"What is your conclusion so far?"

"These areas are connected. The sins aren't traveling by themselves. It's as if they're merged into one. Like they've become an entity."

"You believe the sins have become a living entity? Your presumption I'm assuming?"

"It would explain this more clearly. Besides, the only way for the sins to have merged into an entity, it would need to be brought together by someone of a darker power."

"What of that demon you encountered at Black Raven

Hotel? Could he be responsible for this?"

"Wouldn't surprise me. However, he was keen on something else. Regarding others like myself in the field."

"How would it know of your future to start with? Demons aren't that intelligent when it comes to one's future. The past they're aware of."

"That demon was more powerful than our usual demons. This one claimed to be a lieutenant demon who worked for somebody called Dagor The Soul Eater."

"The Soul Eater?" Donovan jumped. "He hasn't been seen since the Middle Ages."

"Well, if his lieutenant is bumping around the world, he mustn't be hidden anymore."

"Your words are true." Donovan nodded. "Well, once we meet Belinda tomorrow, she'll tag along with us on this case."

"No offense, but, why is she interested in this case? I'm sure she has plenty of cases in this city."

"She wanted this case to work with you again. Though, not as I expect it to be. We're not going to Poveglia this time."

"Noted." Vail stood up from the table. "I'm going to get myself a room in this place. I'll speak to you in the morning."

"Sure thing, Travis. Good night."

"Same to you." Vail left Donovan's hotel room.

While Vail had obtained his own room, he walked down the hallway toward the room. Before he could put the key in, Vail spotted another plague doctor standing at the end of the hall. Cloaked in darkness. Yet, its' beak was glowing. Vail sighed.

"You choose to do this now?" Vail asked. "I would like some kind of answer here."

The doctor kept still. Vail shook his head and rubbed his hands together.

'Guess I'll have to make you."

Vail moved with haste toward the doctor and once he reached him, the doctor had vanished into a thin dark mist. Vail searched the surroundings and found nothing.

"This nonsense is something else."

Vail returned to his room and unlocked the door. He entered and went to sleep.

III

<u>WHAT CAME BETWEEN</u>

The following morning, Travis Vail and Galen Donovan entered a café and inside sitting was Belinda Grazio. They noticed, and Vail only sighed as they approached the table and sat down.

"I know." Belinda said. "You're thrilled to see me again."

"I know why you're here." Vail said. "Besides, that's not why I'm here."

"She's here to assist us on this case."

"I'm aware. So, let's get to it shall we."

"Fair enough." Donovan said. "We need your skills to help us solve this case around the first sins."

"The first sins? That's your case?"

"Can you help us is the question." Vail pointed out. "Can you?"

"I can help. Only if I can come along with the two of you."

"She would do this." Vail said.

"You can."

"*Prego.*" Belinda said. "Glad we can work together again."

"I'm sure you are." Vail said. "Now, can we discuss this case?"

"Yeah. What do you mean by the 'first sins'?" Belinda asked.

"Travis can give you the details. It is his case after all."

"Sure thing. I've come across a number of plague doctors recently and all pf them have some sort of connection to the first sins."

"Like all of them?"

"Yes."

"And you want to find out where these doctors are going and who could be leading them?"

"Precisely. Which is why Galen decided to speak to you. Believing you could be of service to solving this obscure case."

"Well, I can be of service."

"Excellent. Help us and you can go on your way." Vail said.

"What is the plan for today?"

"Since I was visited by a plague doctor last night, I figured we make a trip back to the hotel and search the area. Perhaps, the quiet doctor left something for us to find."

"Well then, I will gather my things and meet you

there."

Vail nodded as Belinda hugged Donovan and left the café. Vail turned to Galen, shaking his head.

"Is it always going to be like this with the two of you?" Donovan asked.

"As long as she focuses on the mission, everything will run smoothly."

"And if not?"

"Then, we will have problems. Delays. Something this job doesn't require us to have."

Vail and Donovan left the café and as they walked down the sidewalk, they stumbled across a pair of street preachers. Dressed in bright colors with the menorah and the Star of David on their clothing. They carried with them signs and a chart, detailing locations of the earth. Vail approached them, glancing at the chart.

"And what is this?"

"What do you think, Esau." The preacher said.

"Heh, Esau now." Vail uttered. "Is that what you just called me?"

"Esau is the white man. You are the Devil!" The Preacher yelled.

"Me the Devil? Look here, fellow, the only one of us who's truly the Devil is you and your gang of deceivers."

"Deceivers?! Read the Word, Esau!"

The Preacher looked, seeing Donovan approaching

them next to Vail. The Preacher's eyes glanced back and forth between Vail and Galen.

"My brother, you can't be hanging around with the enemy."

"The enemy? This man is my friend."

"You can't be friends with Esau, my brother. Look at this chart right here."

Donovan looked at the chart and nodded. Facing the preacher and his brothers-in-arms.

"I have a solution to the problem. Mind if I speak it to you?"

"Yes sir."

"If the white man is truly Esau, then he is your brother."

"What do you mean by that?"

"Esau was born from Isaac's loins. Thereby, Esau is in fact a Hebrew."

"That's not what we're discussing, my brother. The white man is the Devil and the white man is Esau."

"Then, if Esau is the white man and the white man is the Devil, you should get busy at casting the Devil out of him. Free him from the demonic troubles."

The preacher stepped back, grabbing a hold of the Bible in hand. He shook his head.

"We can't help those who's minds have been wiped by the white man. We can't. You're a lost cause, my brother. I am deeply sorry. But, I hope *Yahawashi* has mercy on you and grants you entrance when he returns."

"As do I." Donovan said.

"Heh." Vail chuckled. "Hmm."

The two walked away as the preacher continued his preaching. They turned, entering an alleyway. Vail laughed, and Donovan shook his head.

"Didn't think they would be here." Vail said.

"They're growing. Besides, it's part of the endgame."

"As are many things happening today."

From there, smoke arose from the ground, startling the two. A thick black smoke.

"What is this?" Donovan asked.

"I know who it is."

From the smoke came Kamagrauto, the lieutenant demon. Cloaked in its robe and hood. Its eyes visible from the shadow and its horns spiked out. Kamagrauto levitated over the smoke. His legs could not be seen.

"Travis Vail. Galen Donovan. How intriguing it is to find you both here."

"Is that the demon you talked about?" Donovan asked.

"Yeah. That's him."

Kamagrauto glanced at Vail and Donovan. Its hands held together with his long, sharp, and dirty claws.

"Alright, what do you want?" Vail asked.

"To warn you of your current mission. You will not succeed."

"Is that so?"

"Your future depends on this case and I already know, you will fail. The first sins alone are far too vast for Travis

Vail to solve on his own. You need guidance. Guidance from the other side and I can provide such."

"I understand your nobility. But, me and Galen have this under control."

"Oh, you do?" Kamagrauto gestured. "Then, I will be watching your every move and when you desire my aid and you will, I will make myself known unto you and those who will be at your side when the moment comes."

"What moment?" Vail asked.

"You will know. You will know."

Kamagrauto vanished into the smoke by falling. The darkness cleared from the alleyway and there was nothing remaining.

"That demon is noble?" Donovan asked.

"He has honor. I know. Strange for a demon to possess such a moral trait."

"Well, there are things not even we can comprehend."

"True. But, someday, I hope we can. Right now, we need to go and meet Belinda."

Making their return to the hotel, Belinda waited for them. She saw the looks on their faces.

"What happened?"

"We came across a demon." Donovan said.

"Or the demon came to us." Vail added.

"What kind of demon?"

"The lieutenant kind."

"That's not making any sense, Travis."

"I'm afraid it is true, Belinda. It's the same demon

Travis met at the Black raven Hotel some time ago."

"Kamagrauto? Here?"

"Oh, you know his name." Vail chuckled.

"I thought you were only seeing things. I didn't expect him to exist."

"Well, lass, he exists and trust me, he's not one you would like to meet. Ask Galen of the encounter."

Donovan looked to Belinda and shook his head.

"Kamagrauto is not the typical demons we face. He is something far more ancient and we could feel his power."

"But, do not fret. He offered to help us."

"I hope you refused."

"Not the slightest. He told me whenever I needed his help involving this case, which he is aware of. So, I assume there are others in the spirit world who are familiar with this and aren't giving us any help. Kamagrauto told me to call on him if I needed his aid."

"But, you won't. we'll solve the first sins together."

"True. But, then again, stranger things have happened in this line of work."

Vail walked to the hotel room door.

"I'm going to return to my room and get ready for the work we have to do. I won't be long."

Vail left the room. Belinda turned to Donovan with uncertainty expressing from her face. Galen knew it and sat down.

"What's with him?"

"What do you mean? That's the way he works. Travis is

a very different kind of occult detective."

"Yeah. Not one I would assume to have help from a demon. An ancient one at that."

"Why don't you go and talk to him. See what he tells you."

"He already doesn't want me here."

"And that is more reason for you to talk to him. Get through to him. I know it's possible."

"How so?"

"Because I am the one who trained him in this field. His mentor in a way. Anyway, go and speak with him. It'll give us enough time to prepare to find these plague doctors."

Belinda approached Vail's hotel room door and immediately the door opened. Vail stared at Belinda and she did the same. No words.

"What do you want?" Vail asked.

"Can we talk? For just a second."

Vail sighed as he allowed Belinda into his room. Shutting the door behind, Belinda stood, and Vail walked over to the table and sat down. He gestured his hand toward the other seat. Belinda sat with him.

"What?"

"What's with you?"

"How do you mean?"

"I mean your demeanor, your attitude. What's the problem?"

"There's plague doctors roaming around with the first

sins on their back. I have to find out who's causing this and way."

"That's not what I'm talking about."

"Then I'm confused."

Belinda sighed.

"Why couldn't it have worked between us, Travis? Why didn't you bother to give it a chance?"

"You are not seriously asking me about relationship details right now."

"I am."

"Women always want to talk."

"Only if the men would listen to our words."

"I'm not trying to build up bitterness in my heart, lass. Besides that, I've told you before. A relationship with me won't work."

"Why not?"

"Because when I was young, I was visited by an angel. The angel warned me not to get married. Otherwise, tragedy would follow. Now, I see what the angel meant. Me traveling on this road of life. Dealing with the supernatural daily. Heh, if I did have a wife, she would've most likely divorced me or been killed in the process."

"But, there's always a way."

"Even though you're in this line of work, tragedy still strikes. The fact of Kamagrauto confronting me, proves the angel's point."

"Well, did this angel have a name?"

"He did."

"What was it?"

"Hmm. Michael."

"As in Michael the Archangel."

"Correct. Funny enough, he's been overseeing my activities since I was a little boy. No worries. However, I am keen on the fact he hasn't intervened with my confrontations with Kamagrauto. Maybe time will tell this course."

Vail sighed. Standing up from the chair, he grabbed his coat from the back of the chair, putting it on.

"Now, let's continue this case of ours."

IV

<u>WHAT CAME WITHIN</u>

Vail and Belinda met with Galen, who found the two of them together somewhat odd, but never the case. They moved forward with the case and after studying the trail of the plague doctor that Vail saw, a clue was given. A name connected to a series of plague doctor sightings. Belinda had the name.

"What is it?" Vail asked.

"Here's the name of the recent plague doctor sightings. All from witnesses who've seen the doctors and later a man would come and visit them. Asking about the doctors before they ever went public with a concern."

"The man's name." Donovan said. "What was it?"

"Timothy Ellis."

"Timothy Ellis. I've never heard of him before."

"I have." Vail said. "It's familiar to my ears."

"What do you know of this man, Travis?"

"He's deeply into the spiritual arts. Mystic stuff as well.

But, in the occult circles, he doesn't go by that name. he is known and referred to as Balthazar."

"Is this the mage Balthazar a few have talked about?"

"It is. Balthazar is a mage. A powerful one. Took the name from the biblical magi. Cloaked in his dark-orange hood and robe, he gained power from a deep malevolent force. One of which I am unknown to. But, in time I will find out."

"So, where is Balthazar?" Belinda asked.

"New York City." Vail said. "Which means we have some traveling to do and in little time."

"Yeah, but how long before he finds out we're on to him?"

Vail turned and noticed a shadow hovering in the distance. He stared, and it revealed its eyes.

"Not long." Vail said, staring at the shadow.

"What is it?" Belinda said, turning to also see the shadow.

"What is that?" Donovan asked.

"Balthazar sent him." Vail said. "He already knows."

Vail ran after the shadow without haste.

"Where are you going?!" Belinda yelled.

"I'm going to see what this spirit knows!" Vail answered. "Don't follow me!"

Belinda went to follow, and Donovan held her back.

"Travis can handle himself."

"That's not what I'm worried about."

Vail chased the shadow, leaving Belinda and Donovan

behind. The shadow brought Vail to a spot which was filthy, and the ground was covered in feces and vomit.

"Smells like shit." Vail uttered.

From its appearance, Vail knew it was a spot for homeless people.

"Show yourself, spirit!" Vail yelled.

"In front of him, the shadow appeared. Yet, no fear within it as it morphed into physical form. It resembled a young man, yet he was covered in blood, and chewed on swine's flesh. Vail smirked.

"The hell have we got here. A sin entity."

"Balthazar will have your soul." The entity uttered.

"I think not."

Vail tossed a handful of salt on the entity, startling it. There, Vail began to recite a chant, commanding for the entity to be loosed from Balthazar's hold and to return into the void. The entity was powerful enough to break Vail's chant, forcefully shoving him to the brick wall behind him. Vail fell to the ground and quickly, Kamagrauto arose from the pavement, snatching the entity by the throat and biting it, ripping off its astral head as the body returned to shadow form and fell. Evaporating into thin air.

"I'm not understanding any of this." Vail said.

"You have a higher calling, Travis Vail and I will not allow anyone to turn you away from your cause."

"You know about Balthazar? And how he's behind these plague doctors scaring folks."

"Balthazar has risen up the first sins. Yes. But, there is

another spirit lurking the world. One far more powerful than Balthazar and is on the run from another soul as we speak."

"I wish that particular soul the best in his endeavors. Could use the bit of the help every now and then. How come you didn't tell me all this before I went further?"

"I know many things. Things even the smartest man would tremble at the sound."

"Good thing, I'm not the smartest man. I'm just an exorcist."

"One with a higher purpose."

"Then, why don't you just travel onto New York City and stop Balthazar for me? That way, I can focus more on this 'higher purpose'."

'Because it is not my duty to finish your work. You started this case, you must finish it."

Vail chuckled.

"I'll be. You know your kind are some slick sons of bitches."

"Do not compare me to the common demons you've slain."

"I'm not." Vail asked. "But, you really are a strange demon, lad."

"I am not like those demons. I am Kamagrauto. Kamagrauto."

Kamagrauto vanished into the black smoke as before. Vail shrugged himself and scoffed.

V

<u>WHAT CAME ABOUT</u>

Vail returned to Belinda and Galen, who saw his tiredness and often slackly behavior after things have arisen. They approached him with concern and he only smiled.

"What happened to the shadow?" Donovan asked.

"It was taken care of."

"How?" Belinda wondered.

"Kamagrauto killed it."

"The demon Kamagrauto?"

"Yes, Galen. The same demon we met in the alleyway. I confronted the damn thing. By the way, the shadow was a sin entity."

"That can't be so?" Donovan said. "there hasn't been one of them since the World Wars."

"And yet, here it is and not out of curiously either. Balthazar conjured it up."

"What happened to the spirit, Travis?" Belinda asked.

"I nearly came close to casting it away, but it possessed a

power that outweigh my voice and tossed me against the wall. After that, Kamagrauto appeared and decapitated the spirit. Good for me."

"The demon helped you?" Donovan asked. "It killed the spirit right in front of your eyes?"

"Yes. Afterwards we spoke, and he revealed to me he's been aware of this whole case the entire time. I scoffed and wondered how come he couldn't do the work for us. Said it wasn't in his purpose. However, Balthazar is the one behind all of this and there's another sin spirit roaming the earth. But, Kamagrauto confirmed to me that another individual is chasing that spirit right now. So, hopefully we won't have too much work on our hands."

"So, what is our current objective?" Belinda asked.

"Galen, call Colton, tell him to meet us in New York. We need to confront Balthazar now and fast before more of his little ideas manifest into reality."

Vail, Belinda, and Donovan made their travels and arrived in New York City. Prepared to meet Balthazar. Wherever he may reside.

VI

<u>WHAT CAME TO BE</u>

Vail, Belinda, and Donovan stood in Times Square. Seeing the crowds go by, walking about their business. Galen shook his head in shame.

"They're just coming and going."

"It's their nature, Galen. Besides, it proves we're not the ones trapped in Pop Culture and materialism."

"Now, where will Colton be?" Belinda asked.

"He should be around here somewhere."

Vail looked out, not seeing his ally. Later, he turned his head and from there, he managed to get a glance at Colton. He pointed.

"He's coming this way."

Colton Levi approached them and shook hands. Standing in the middle of Times Square mind you amid the roaming crowds.

"Good to see you." Vail said. "Now, why did you want us to meet you out here?"

"Because, the guy you're looking for oftentimes roams through here."

"Are you sure?"

"Plague doctors are seen continually here. It's looked at as just a cosplay show."

"Point us in the direction." Vail said.

They followed Colton through the Square, moving past the crowds. There, Vail and Galen noticed a group of street preachers, yelling at all the white men in the crowds. Vail scoffed as the argument escalated to a brawl.

"They're everywhere."

"It's part of the times, Travis." Donovan said.

"True one."

Colton had led them into a spot where they set shops. He pointed toward the spot which had a crescent moon carved on the door.

"Is this the spot?" Belinda asked.

"It certainly is." Vail confirmed. "Let's see what's inside."

They entered the shop and quickly, surrounded by plague doctors. They raised up their guards as the doctors stood quirt and still.

"Oh, this is the place." Vail said.

The doctors approached them and suddenly, took steps back. Moving in a fashioned line on each side, leading them further into the shop down a hallway. They walked down the hallway and they reached a room. In the room were images of occult symbols, sacrifices, and spells. A pentagram was carved into the wooden floor. Vail stepped forward, seeing a hooded man crouched down at the fire.

"Stand up, you're embarrassing yourself here." Vail said.

The hooded man stood up, removing his hood. Revealing himself to be Balthazar. Vail smiled. Pointing.

"You son of a bitch!" Vail laughed.

"Travis Vail. The Spirit-Seeker."

"In the flesh."

"I figured you would come."

"Had not choice, lad. I've come to stop your doings. Raising up plague doctors and spirits. The shit has to stop."

"It will not cease until my work is complete."

"Your work is done. Just let it all go. Quit working for the enemy and just retire."

Balthazar raised his hands, shoving Belinda, Galen, and Colton to the floor. Holding them in place with a sort of spiritual bind. Only he and Vail remained standing.

"Why are you doing this?"

"Because I have a master to praise. One who granted me these gifts. I must serve him with all my might."

"Then, your master has to deal with me. And others out there."

"My master's coming was already thwarted by someone. I will not allow the Cryptic Zone to remain shut. He will rise."

"No, he won't."

"And what will you do when he rises and comes for

you?”

“Don’t all malevolent forces come for me? It’s my job to piss your kind off.”

“How about a deal.”

“A what now?”

“A deal. You leave me to my work and I let your friends live.”

“Um, deal declined. However, I can offer you a deal.”

“Like so?”

“Let my friends go or find yourself entering Hell a little early than you expected.”

“You cannot kill me.” Balthazar declared. “No man can murder me!”

“I’m not going to murder you. I’m simply going to offer you a trip. Besides, best you deal with me and not Kamagrauto.”

Balthazar froze. His eyes went wider.

“Kamagrauto?” Balthazar asked.

“Yes. You know, lieutenant demon. Works for Dagor the Soul Eater. That kind of guy. He knows of your work by the way. Told me of it. Raising the first sins and all. Plague doctors and such. He knows. And if he knows, who’s the say the others know as well.”

Balthazar shook, dropping the hold on Belinda, Galen, and Colton. Vail smirked.

“They will not have me.” Balthazar said. “My master will protect me!”

“Then, let’s see him protect you from this.”

Vail raised up his hand, shoving Balthazar down. He began to chant and before he could start, a whirlwind of blue flames surrounded Balthazar. Taking him away. The room was silent. Galen approached the spot. Belinda and Colton were confused.

"The hell just happened?" Colton asked.

"His master took him." Vail said.

"What of the first sins?" Belinda asked. "What of the doctors?"

"We'll see if they still stand." Donovan said.

They returned to the entrance, discovering the doctors are gone. Vail knew Balthazar's fear had driven the doctors and the first sins away. He smirked as they left the shop. The case was done. Yet, Balthazar was somewhere in the world. Possibly in other realms of existence. Vail knew he would see him again down the road.

With everyone returning to their proper places, Vail sat inside his own domain, researching more on the sin entity Kamagrauto mentioned in their conversation. There, Vail discovered there's an ancient power had risen, which is the cause for the sin entity's presence.

"In my line of work, things happen for the worst. Usually the better."

He knew the power was far too great for himself to face. By that standard, Vail went to visit a friend. A friend in Washington D.C.

TRAVIS VAIL, SPIRIT-SEEKER: LOST GIRLS AND FOUND

I

<u>ANOTHER LOST GIRL</u>

Travis Vail sat at his desk, looking over the cases which have been reported ever since the conflicts with Balthazar, the Sin Phantom, and Demonticronto. Vail remembered his encounters with the other supernatural forces. He chuckled under his breath memorizing their allegiance for the moment. He looked over as his cell phone began to vibrate.

"Who's calling?" Vail answered.

Vail listened and he listened closely. He nodded, taking out a pen and writing down the information. He nodded, ending the call. He looked at what he wrote and shook his head.

"Guess it's begun again."

He grabbed his gear, put on his coat and left. Sometime later, Vail arrived in the town where the call had come.

"Back in Chesterfield." Vail sighed. "Let's see what's happening here."

While in Chesterfield, Vail searched for the caller. The caller left an address for Vail to find. Which he traced, finding the address to be in the suburbs. A quiet neighborhood. Vail saw several children playing with each other in a field across the street. Others rode their bikes down the road. Confused, he found the address and approached the home's front door. Vail knocked. The door answered and Vail was surprised.

"Cooper Lawrence?" Vail said.

"Good to see you again, Mr. Vail."

"Wait, you're the one who called?"

"I am."

"But why? What's happened?"

"Come in and we'll explain everything."

"Certainly."

Inside the home, Cooper's wife, Janice saw Vail and she went to greet him. Sitting in the living room was Carrie. Vail saw her and she saw him.

"She's gotten older over the past few years, hasn't she?" Vail said.

"I'm not a child anymore." Carrie said.

"How old are you now? Fifteen? Sixteen?"

"I'm sixteen."

"You're not getting into any trouble, are you?"

"None of a major issue."

"Ah." Vail mumbled."

He turned back to her parents with a concerned, yet unworried look.

"Why did you call me?"

"Please come with us. We'll explain in private."

Vail nodded and followed Carrie's parents into Cooper's office. Once Vail had entered, Cooper closed the door as Vail sat down in front of the desk. Janice sat next to him while Cooper sat behind the desk. Vail was still confused, looking back and forth between Cooper and Janice.

"Why did you call me? I'm not understanding what's happening here."

"We called you because it's starting again." Janice said.

"What's starting again?"

"Carrie's been speaking to someone in her room."

"You're sure it's not just a friend of hers. Perhaps a lad she met at school?"

"No." Cooper said. "That was we thought. Until we overheard her say the name, Leta."

Vail sat back in the chair. Quiet within himself. Leta had returned? Vail was unsure of the possibility.

"Are you sure we're talking about the same Leta? The one who possessed your daughters all those years ago?"

"We're certain." Janice said. "We've never met any of Carrie's friend who have that name."

"You believe Leta is trying to continue what she started?"

"Yes. Why bother our daughter when she's done nothing wrong. She's a good kid."

"That's the thing, Cooper. Good children are often the targets for such spirits."

"So, will you do what you did before?" Janice questioned. "I'm positive it will cleanse her again."

"I will try. But I must be sure of all of this. Carrie's older now and the connection could be deeper than before. I cannot risk anything of importance. Carrie's life depends on it."

"Thank you." Janice replied.

"Please, do what you can." Cooper added.

"I will."

Vail left the home and went to the library, as per usual.

113

II

<u>REMEMBERING THE ONE BEFORE</u>

Travis Vail sat by himself in the library, reading up on the same files as before. He closed the books and pulled out his phone, dialing a number. On the other end was Raynard Brown. Vail had begun to tell him of Leta's possible return and the connection she has with Carrie Lawrence. Raynard refereed him to search the home's land once more to find anything unusual that may pertain toward the Lost Girl spirit.

"I will do that, Raynard. Just to be sure."

Vail hanged up and left the library, returning to the Lawrence home. While walking back to his car, he saw a homeless man sitting on the sidewalk beside the library. He was cloaked in a black hooded jacket from his shoulders to his knees. He walked with a hunch in his back and frail in his steps. Vail nodded toward him and the man stood up, approaching him. His hands were out and Vail grinned.

"I would give you something if I had anything. I'm sorry."

"Don't be sorry, Spirit-Seeker."

"Pardon?"

The man raised his head up, facing Vail. He stepped

114

back, seeing the homeless man's face. He was old, very old. His long white beard was stretched outward and his eyes were near dim.

"How do you know who I am?" Vail questioned.

"I've been around for a very long time. I've seen those of your kind for many centuries do the work you're doing this day."

"Who are you?"

"I'm only a wanderer, Spirit-Seeker. I come and I go."

"A wanderer? From what part of the world?"

"A place far from here. Across the pond you could say."

"East lands, huh. I see. Well, I need to get going."

"As you shall. For I am aware of the task set before you. The Lost Girl has returned. Hasn't she? Attempting to bond with another host?"

"So I've been told. I'll stop her for good this time."

"I'm sure you will. But, take heed to these words. Her connection with the young girl isn't as simple as you would assume it to believed. For when a spirit goes out of one, it indeed returns much stronger and with friends of its own."

"I know the works. No need to repeat them to me."

"Of course. Now, you will see them in action. Take care, Spirit-Seeker."

Vail nodded, waving away as he turned to his car. He looked back and the man was gone.

"Every time."

III

THE STRANGE CASE OF LETA AND CARRIE

Vail returned to the Lawrence home, seeing Janice running out of the home toward him with Cooper behind.

"What's going on?" Vail asked.

"It's Carrie." Janice said. "There's something wrong with her."

'Wait here. I'll go look to her."

Vail ran into the home, seeing Carrie standing in the living room completely still. Her hair moved smoothly as if the wind was within the home. Vail couldn't feel it as he approached her.

"Carrie, whatever she has on you, you must fight it."

Carrie did not move. Her hands twitched but could not bend. Her fingers were straightened. As if there was electricity holding them in place. Vail took another step forward and Carrie's head turned toward him in a quick rush. Her eyes were solid black, and she grinned. Vail sighed.

"You're not Carrie."

"I am not."

"Leta, release her from your control. Now."

"You believe this will end as it did before? I have learned much since our last encounter."

"I'm sure you have. Still bothering this young girl with your agendas for control."

"We share a bond. A bond that you broke."

"You don't belong here, spirit."

"Your words will not save Carrie this time. I have grown in such spiritual power since the last departure."

"You will leave Carrie and you will be gone for good."

"Make your move. Spirit-Seeker."

Vail reached into his pocket, taking out his book used in many of his cases. He began to recite a page and while doing such, Leta let out a great laugh. The laugh irritated Vail to the point where his reciting had ceased, and he could not utter the words. Vail immediately felt powerless, seeing Leta had truly grown in the spiritual arts. Peculiar for a spirit in Vail's words. Vail had no other options in his place. He paused himself, seeing the black eyes on Carrie and the laughter of Leta coming from her mouth.

"I know." Vail whispered. "I know what I have to do."

Vail placed the book into his jacket pocket, pointed toward Leta while walking back to the door.

"This is far from over."

"Where are you going?!"

"I have something in mind to get rid of you."

"You believe you can cast me away? After what I've just shown you?!"

"Not me. I know a guy and I'll be back with him on my side. And hers."

"I cannot let you leave."

"You will if you let Carrie have control of her body. When I return, then you can rise up and face me. Then, we'll see who will remain."

"Are you challenging me? Using this young girl as a tool for your works?"

"Truth be told, who's the tool in this story? It's not Carrie."

Vail walked back outside, seeing Cooper and Janice waiting in a slight panic mode. Janice ran up to him with tears in her eyes.

"Is she alright?!"

"Unfortunately, Leta has possession over your daughter."

"Aren't you going to do what you did the last time?"

"I tried. Didn't work."

"Then, what are you planning on doing, Mr. Vail?" Cooper asked.

"I know a guy who can help me with this case. Leta's become far stronger than the last time. I'll need some assistance with this one."

Vail walked to his car before turning back to the Lawrences.

"By the way, your daughter should be back to her senses. Leta would have left knowing what I'm planning on doing. Keep an eye on her until I return."

Vail left the Lawrence home. Traveling nearly afar off into the outskirts, stumbling upon an old building. Vail exited his car, approaching the building. The structure was pre-Civil War, yet with a mixture of medieval architecture. Vail nodded.

"This is the spot."

Vail walked up to the large double-doors and knocked.

After a second knock, the doors open. Yet, Vail saw no one. He shrugged his shoulders and entered the building with the doors shutting behind him. The closing of the doors did not faze nor concern him. Vail continued walking forward, finding himself standing in a large room near a corridor.

"Hey, I know you're here." Vail said. "So, do us a favor and come on out."

Vail turned around, seeing a large window and hovering at the window was a silhouette of a figure, levitating in the air. Vail smirked, crossing his arms.

"I know who you are." Vail said.

The figure moved forward toward Vail, as he did not move himself. the figure came into the light and revealed itself to be Doctor Donald Fortune. Vail applauded.

"I knew this was your spot all along."

"One of many." Fortune said. "Why are you here, Travis Vail, Spirit-Seeker?"

"You're aware of my work?"

"I know everything that pertains to the mystic realms which surround our world."

"That's nice. Look, I need your help. It's a major concern."

"My help? Why?"

"There's a young girl. She's possessed by a spirit. A powerful spirit. I need your help in breaking the soul tie between them."

"Last I read, you call on the one who's words you read from your book. Didn't you at least try that?"

"I worked last time. Leta's grown more powerful since then."

"Leta." Fortune said. "The Lost Girl spirit."

"Yes. You've heard of her?"

"I've dealt when her kind before. Just not Leta herself."

"She's become stronger after I sent her away. I'm not sure how."

"You're telling me you were the one who sent her away those years ago?"

"I am. I was younger and much of a novice in those days. But, I did what needed to be done to save the girl."

"Now, Leta's retuned to the same girl and has an even stronger hold on her?"

"That's correct."

"I understand."

Fortune opened the doors of the building to the outside. Vail looked back and forth to the door and to Fortune.

"Aren't you going to tell me what to do? I need to break the soul tie between them."

"Yes, you do." Fortune replied. "However, I will not allow you to go alone."

"Why can't you just tell me what to do? I can deal with Leta myself."

"I need to see this Leta in person. Learn her motives. That way, I can prepare myself and my apprentice in case she returns again in the future."

"Your apprentice? There's no one else here."

"He's preoccupied on a task afar off. Now, are you ready to save this girl?"

"After you."

"I'll meet you there."

"Wait a second, fellow. You don't even know where she is."

"I'll follow your lead. You drove out here after all. You can drive back."

"Can't you just teleport us there. And the car?"

"I can. But, should I?"

"It would prove much faster and speed is what we'll need to get rid of Leta."

"Very true. Stand still."

"Ok. Why-"

IV

<u>A STUBBORN SPIRIT ENTERS THE PIT</u>

Within a sudden moment, Vail and Fortune were standing in front of the Lawrence home. Vail looked around, seeing the home and even his car. He turned to Fortune, who only nodded.

"How'd you do that?"

"The Orb of Quirinto." Fortune answered, showing the org attached to the amulet around his neck. Glowing with mystical energy.

"Where did you get it?"

"A long story not worth telling at the moment. We need to get Leta out of the girl."

"Agreed."

"I'm assuming she's inside." Fortune said.

"Let's go in then."

They approached the door of the home with Janice opening it as soon as she saw Vail. Cooper ran up behind her, confused about Fortune's appearance.

"Mr. Vail, who's the friend?"

"He's going to help me save your daughter."

"Who is he supposed to be?" Janice asked. "Some kind of magician."

"Sorcerer, madam."

"We assumed Vail could handle this on his own." Cooper mentioned. "Like the last time."

"This isn't like the last time." Vail replied. "Leta has a much stronger hold on Carrie. Doctor Fortune is here to aid me in setting your daughter free."

"Is your friend capable of this kind of work?"

"I've faced much more and far worse than a possession. I'm skilled enough."

Cooper nodded, allowing Fortune to enter the home. Upon entering, Fortune saw Carrie's body levitating above the living room floor. Vail entered, seeing the levitation.

"She's getting stronger."

"We have this under control." Fortune said. "I desire to speak with Leta."

Carrie's body moved around in the air as her head turned toward Fortune's gaze and her eyes were locked on. Still black. She grinned heavily, starting Carrie's parents.

"Vail, you've returned. And I see you didn't come alone."

"I did not."

Fortune stepped forward as a gust of wind rustled from Carrie's body, shoving him and Vail back. Fortune twirled his arms and the wind ceased. Vail noticed the tactic and shrugged his shoulders.

"That's convenient."

"Who are you?" Leta's voice asked.

"I am Doctor Donald Fortune. Supreme Enchanter of the mystical realm and I have been brought here to rid you of this young girl and of this material world."

"Supreme Enchanter? Another one?"

"She's familiar with your kind." Vail noticed. "Are you

sure you can handle this, Fortune?"

"I am positive." Fortune clapped his hands together with the energy covering them. "Prepare to do your part in this, Spirit-Seeker."

"My part?"

"Do what you've done before. I will handle the rest."

Vail turned to Carrie's parents. Telling them to go outside and wait until the work is done. They agreed with tears in their eyes as the left the house. Vail turned his focus back toward Leta, while Fortune began levitating just a few feet off the ground. Leta had full control over Carrie's body, now posing it against Fortune. Vail slowly reached into his pocket, grabbing his book.

"Do you have what you need?" Fortune asked.

"I do."

"Then you're ready."

"I am."

Leta rushed toward Fortune as he stretched forth his arms, creating a barrier between himself and Leta. Vail was in the middle of the barrier with his book opened. Fortune looked toward him and nodded. Vail started to recite from the book the same words as before. Leta's focus was not on Vail, but on Fortune as she tried beating down the mystic barrier. She screamed with rage, punching the barrier. Fortune kept his demeanor. Focused and in control as Vail continued reading.

"Add one more to the speech." Fortune told Vail. "And speak it in something other than Latin."

"I got it." Vail replied. "*Tam qate alhabl alfidiya baynak wabaynaha alan!*"

Leta turned to Vail as he closed the book. Her eyes began to show the pupils as she struggled to hold herself and Carrie together. Her body was fighting between staying levitated and coming down to the floor. She glared toward Fortune as he could see Carrie's eyes starting to appear and Leta's power decreasing.

"You heard him, Lost Girl. The soul tie is broken. Leave. Now."

Fortune clapped his hands and the barrier collapsed as Leta let out a great scream. Carrie's body floated and fell to the floor, not before Vail could catch her. Fortune cleared the home of any residue of Leta's power. About thirty minutes later, Carrie's parents entered the home to find Carrie laying down in her room on the bed.

"Is she alright?" Janice asked.

"She's well." Vail said. "Leta is gone."

"Oh. Thank you. Thank you both."

Fortune nodded. Cooper approached the two and shook their hands. Thanking them for their help. Vail wanted to wait for Carrie to wake up and once she did, he spoke to her with Fortune standing by. Carrie told Vail that she was aware of everything that was happening. She stated she no longer feels the connection she shared with Leta. But, she told him that she could also see Leta's intentions. Her intentions were dire, and she was brought forth by a sorcerer who saw fit to distract Vail from some grander plan.

"Don't concern yourself with our affairs." Vail said. "We're just glad you're alright."

Afterwards, Vail said his goodbyes, hoping he doesn't have to return due to such similar events. Later, Vail spoke with Fortune about Carrie's words and he understood them greatly. Fortune warned Vail about an opposing adversary of his to which Vail stated he had no adversaries. Balthazar could be counted as one, but not a great adversary.

"I'm referring to anyone you met in your early years." Fortune said. "Someone who was very peculiar to your work. Like an opposite of the coin."

Vail thought, "There was one, however I haven't seen him since the investigation."

"I see. Meanwhile, you should keep an eye out. Just in case."

"One more thing." Vail said. "Why did you tell me not to speak the words in Latin?"

"Because you have to get outside of your box when confronting these matters. Spirits such as Leta keep memories, you know."

"Informative of you."

"Arabic was an interesting choice."

"It's the first one that came to mind."

"Good to hear. Just keep watch. All that Carrie told you, do not forget it."

"I will keep it all in mind. Thank you for the assistance, Doctor."

"It was a necessary duty."

Fortune warped the surroundings into a portal back to his true residence, the Citadel of Enchantment. Vail saw the large structure and how it was placed amongst the trees in a wilderness afar off. Vail smirked.

"That's where you reside."

"Indeed. I will be seeing you around, Travis Vail."

"Until next time."

"We'll see, Spirit-Seeker."

Fortune entered the portal and was gone. Vail took in

the moment before entering his car and driving away, mediating on all that transpired. While on the road, Vail accepted the though in his heart and mind that Leta was gone. For good this time. To him, it was a great victory for the living.

127

I

ROME OF THE WEST

On a cold and sunny day in St. Louis, Missouri, Travis Vail had entered the gates to the city. Vail's purpose of arriving in the city was due to a call he received from his mentor, Dr. Galen Donovan about a proposed haunting moving through a particular region of the city. Vail had once driven through St. Louis in the past, yet he never stayed nor wondered if the city had any haunting to it. Demons? Sure. But, the occasional haunting? Never lingered in the mind of the Spirit-Seeker.

Vail drove through the city, arriving at the Central Library. Walking inside as he saw Donovan and his colleague, Colton Levi sitting at a table. They saw Vail approaching and stood up to greet their friend. Sitting down after their greeting, Vail was immediately interested in the case. His expression could be seen by nearing everyone in the library. Galen smiled.

"You're eager to know more aren't you?" Colton asked.

"In a way, I am." Vail smirked. "So, what's happening in this place?"

"Hauntings of history." Galen answered. "Those affected have said to have seen glimpses into the past and the future."

"You're serious?"

"Serious as can be." Colton said. "The people we talked to said they saw glimpses of Ancient Rome."

"Fitting." Vail replied. "Seeing as how we're in the Rome of the West. Makes a connection in a way."

"That's not all." Galen said. "While some saw the past in just landmarks, others saw events. Events such as the burning of the Library of Alexandria, wars of the Crusades, even the parting of the Red Sea."

Vail nodded.

"Well then, they had the opportunity of seeing spectacles. One thing I must ask. What you're both telling me are events which connect to the past. What about those who have seen the future?"

"One man we spoke to said he saw the future. Countries we know of today no longer existed. Soldiers were automated and humanity was changed completely."

"I know the telling. But, how is this connected to the supernatural? From what I've gathered by your information, these glimpses could be the simple workings of a sage, fortune teller, or even some kind of techno-geek. It's all technology based is what I can tell."

"He has a point, Dr. Donovan." Colton said.

"He does. Well, that's all we can give you. I'm sure you want to know if there's a history on this."

"There has to be. Besides, we're in a museum. Isn't there something here that may connect all of this. Besides the artifacts."

"While you were arriving into the city, Raynard went to

the Central Library to do some studying. Perhaps you'll want to meet with him there. See what he uncovers."

"As I always do." Vail stood up from the table. "Are you two staying in town or are you leaving already?"

"Do you need our help on this one?" Colton asked. "Or are you other friends here elsewhere?"

Vail gave them a look. They knew the look and grinned.

"My 'friends' as you call them, are dealing with their own matters elsewhere. Besides, I'm sure you'll meet them eventually."

"I'm intrigued to meet this Doctor you've encountered. They call him the Supreme Enchanter, right?"

"It's a lineage title." Vail said. "Nothing more to me."

"Contact me when you've solved it." Galen replied.

"I will."

Vail left the museum and traveled to the Central Library where he found Raynard Brown, his trusty historian going through the books. Connecting the dots to the case. He raised up his head to see Vail standing in front of him, grinning.

"You could've said something."

"I thought about that. But, I wouldn't disturb a man such as you in your work. Could cause a stumble."

Raynard took a moment to step away from the books to greet Vail with a handshake and hug. Bringing him over to the table stacked with books, Vail could tell Raynard had been busy for a while.

"Galen told me you would be here." Vail said.

"Anytime a library is near and case is discovered, it is my place to work."

"Speaking of the case. Have you found anything related to these glimpses through time?"

Raynard grabbed one book. A book detailed in the history of Missouri. Flipping through the pages, he told Vail about the history of the state, more so the history of the city. Primarily detailing the Lemp Neighborhood. Vail took note of it, writing details down in a notepad.

"You're writing things down now?" Raynard said to his surprise.

"Yeah. Have any of the witnesses to the case been through the neighborhood?"

"No. this neighborhood the usual when it comes to the paranormal?"

"The ghosts and the like?"

"Yes."

"Very well. I'll keep that in mind once I come back around to the city. Right now, this whole time case is needed to be solved."

Raynard nodded.

"I did come up with a location related to all the witnesses."

"Where is this place? In the city or outside of it?"

"It's in the city. How else do you expect to have so many witnesses to this case."

"You know how these things go. Strange things always occur outside of the city. Especially cities like this one."

"The Cathedral Basilica of St. Louis. It's over in Central West End region of the city."

"Of all the places I would've thought. The Cathedral was low on my list."

Raynard grinned.

"What were you expecting it to be? The Arch?"

"It fits in this scenario, does it not. Even the Science Center would be a proper place for a time mystery."

Putting the notepad inside his coat pocket, Vail had everything he needed to move on with the case.

"I'll head to the place tonight." Vail said. "Keep my appearance from the public is best."

"I'm sure you will. Although, I'm not certain if the Archbishop will be there."

"In the late hours of the night?"

"Could be possible."

Vail kept that in mind and nodded with a smirk.

Vail shook Raynard's hand and took his leave from the library.

II

<u>INNER BEINGS</u>

Once the night had fallen over St. Louis, Travis Vail arrived at the Cathedral silently. Entering through the front doors with ease seemed a bit unusual for him. However, Vail had entered the cathedral and what threw him off for a moment was the detail of the place. Vail stood inside the main aisle, gazing at the ceiling and the walls. He nodded.

"Nice work they've put in this place."

Vail looked ahead down the aisle and saw what he believed to be a disembodied figure hovering. Moving with speed, Vail ran down the aisle toward the shadow and before he could even get a hand near it, the shadow evaporated with a faint spark of red light. Vail stopped himself as the lights within the cathedral began to flicker. A grin formed upon his face.

"This is what I was expecting." Vail said as he turned around to find himself staring at the figure, fully embodied at the other end of the aisle.

Vail stared at the figure and the details which grabbed him was the attire of the figure. It was dressed just like himself. Black trench coat, white buttoned shirt, black slacks and shoes. It even had a trimmed beard and mustache like Vail.

"Didn't know there were spirits that seemed to like my fashion." Vail scoffed. "I'm flattered. Now, tell me your name and why you're here."

The figure said nothing. Vail took that as a notion of talk and continued to ask more questions. The figure replied to nothing. Seeing as how talking wasn't moving the conversation along, Vail proceeded to walk down the aisle toward the figure and as he walked, the stench in the air caught him. Stumbling him in his own steps. Shaking his head and covering his nose.

"The hell is that?!"

A grin grew on the figure's shadowed face and Vail realized the stench. His eyes told the story.

"Sulfur. You're a demon, aren't you."

The figure let out a sigh which sounded similar to a growl. Vail continued to walk closer to the figure and after the next step, the figure moved forward into the light for Vail to see. Inching closer, the figure was engulfed in the light and Vail was paused.

"You've got to be shitting me." Vail said with a sigh.

The figure was indeed Vail himself. Yet, with a slight difference. Its face pale and slightly charred. The clothing torn and burnt. The demon showed its fangs toward Vail to Vail's slight humor.

"Ah. Now I get it." Vail said. "You're my demonic counterpart. I've heard of your kind before. I guess everyone has a doppelganger such as yourself. Never thought I would meet my own. Yet, ah the hell with it. What are you doing to this city?"

"I've done nothing." The demon answered. "I've come for you."

"Or you have, eh? Well then. I'm right here."

The demon chuckled as its hands were consumed by fire. The burning of the flames increased the stench of sulfur in the church. Vail fanned his hands to avoid the smell and chuckled under his breath. The demon charged the flames toward Vail in the form of fireballs. Vail ducked quickly to avoid the scorching attack.

"You wanna play." Vail shook his hands, conjuring fire in his own hands. "Let's play."

The two Vails began a battle of wits with fire. Throwing balls of fire toward one another to each own's deflecting. Vail twirled his hands, circling the fire in the air and shoving the circle of fire toward the demon. The demon took the circle for its own use, returning it to Vail in the form of a blast. Vail raised up his hands, conjuring an energy shield, deflecting the blowing flame. The two continued their attacks toward one another as sparks from the flames bounced against the walls of the church.

"You don't give up, I see." Vail chuckled. "We're alike. Aside from the appearance."

Vail gave another spin with his hands, forming a conjunction of the two flames and blasting it into his demonic doppelganger. The blast pushed the demonic Vail through the doors to the outside. Vail rushed out to see the entity and found him laying flat on the ground. A second passed and he rose up. Eyes black as the night sky.

"Typical." Vail smirked.

Lunging to his feet with a snarl, the demonic entity went for a strike until it quickly vanished into a puff of sulfur. Vail stood still. Confused to his doppelganger's disappearance. He sighed.

"Well, that was unexpected."

"Is it?" A echoing voice spoke from behind Vail.

Turning back and looking inside the church, Vail returned inside as he saw at the podium Kamagrauto. The doors behind Vail closed to his dismay as Kamagrauto greeted him. Vail waved slightly before shaking his head.

III

<u>OLD CONFRONTATIONS</u>

"Just who I was expecting." Vail said. "I figure you would be here for something important."

"I came just in time. You know you're not capable of holding back your demonic doppelganger for long."

"I was doing just fine before you arrive. No worries from me."

"But I did come for an important cause."

"I believe you." Vail said while sitting down on the front pew while Kamagrauto remained hovering in front of the podium.

"So, what is the cause you're come for? I hope it concerns myself being in this city. The reason of the matter."

"It does."

"Oh. How good."

"Blessings come in many ways, Spirit-Seeker."

"Yeah. I'm aware. Now, what do you know about what's been happening here?"

"The cause of these time anomalies is the doings of an old adversary of yours."

"Old adversary?" Vail paused. "Well, for certain, I know this isn't the work of Vernon Lance. It's not sinister enough. Can't be Leta. Not her style. I'm not sure who you're referring to."

"You do not remember?"

"Listen, I've come across many malevolent figures. Not all of them retain their names in my mind. Just their attributes of power. Mostly."

"Ugh. I guess you want me to let out the name of the one responsible."

"Might as well. I can still go through with the list of names of the ones I've encountered."

"No need for that. The one responsible for the causes in this city is Balthazar."

Vail paused himself. His eyes shifting back and forth as his mind wandered.

"Balthazar? The same fellow who fled our last encounter some time ago?"

"What other Balthazar do you know of?"

"Not many to be honest with you."

"His workings with the darker forces have provided him a new skill set of shifting time itself. Allowing elements of the past to interfere with the affairs of the present and the distractions through the future."

Vail sighed as he stood up from the pew, gazing around the cathedral.

"Then, what am I waiting for. Where is the fellow now?"

"He's occupied at the Gateway Arch as we speak."

"The Gateway Arch? Why? Ah. Never mind. I get it."

Vail made his way toward the exit and before taking another step, he turned back to Kamagrauto.

"I'm assuming you'll be there?"

"You know me by now, Spirit-Seeker. I'm always

around.”

After his words touched the air, he vanished from the cathedral to Vail’s humorous dismay. Shrugging his shoulders as calm as he is, he exited the cathedral.

139

IV

<u>ACROSS TIME AND SPACE</u>

While Vail made his arrival at the Arch, he was quickly caught by the flowing energy coming from beneath the Arch. He knew it was Balthazar as he stepped out of his car and saw the hooded figure twirling his arms in the air above his head.

"Every time." Vail said.

Balthazar, shrouded his blood-red hood and cloak continued to twirl and spin his arms as his fingers fluttered like electricity in front of the Arch. Vail made his steps quiet to the surprise from the fleeing civilians who sought to avoid the powerful energy. Vail had reached nearly ten feet from Balthazar and stopped.

"Still at this?" Vail yelled through the rushing sound of the energy.

Balthazar's arms froze as his head slowly turned around to gaze toward the Spirit-Seeker. Their eyes touched and a hint of fear grasped the throat of Balthazar.

"Travis Vail?! How? Why?!"

"How am I here? Fully story actually. I heard there had been some time warps happening in this city. Figured it was all caused by some typical supernatural threat. Yet, I've discovered with the help of a friend that it was only you and you alone. To be honest, I'm slightly disappointed."

"This is the problem between you and I."

"What's that?"

"You've never taken me seriously. None of you have."

"Because you only copy what others have done. You've never achieved something on your own to simply call your own."

Balthazar chuckled.

"That is where you're wrong."

"I'm wrong?"

"With the power of this darker force consuming the earth, I have managed to achieve a feat none of you have been capable of doing. I have the power to cross time itself. To bring the past and future to the present. To see the things which have happened and the things yet to come."

"I take it reading history books wasn't enough for you. Much less waiting for the future to happen."

"You don't understand! I can travel to any point in time. See any event and I can alter it to my will. I can make sure you and your allies were never born."

"I've heard that before. Not impressed."

"But, I will let you in on one secret I've uncovered before I kill you."

"Go ahead and speak it. You're getting a little boring."

"Not only can I travel across time. I can travel to other universes. Universes outside of our own. Places yet to be seen. Worlds yet to conquer."

Vail took a moment to step back.

"Universes? I'm not sure you want to trouble them, Balthazar. You may come across someone who won't take you as lightly as I am right now."

Balthazar's hands flashed and was consumed by the same glowing white energy from the Arch. A grin formed upon his face as even his eyes shined like the energy.

"I guess I'll have to show you."

Balthazar stretched his arms, blasting the energy toward Vail as he jumped out of its path. Down on the ground, Vail rose up and conjured up several balls of fire and threw them into Balthazar's chest, shoving him back near the Arch as the energy continued to pour through. The attacks between the two continued until Vail looked up near the Arch and saw Kamagrauto.

"Knock him in." Kamagrauto yelled.

Vail looked as Balthazar wiped the flames from his clothing and his closeness toward the Arch. Shrugging his shoulders, Vail ran and speared Balthazar as the two entered the energy, quickly transporting themselves through a wormhole of stars, water, fire, and earth. Flowing through the wormhole, Balthazar continued his attacks as Vail deflected the energy blast with a shield of his own making. Vail retailed with a blast of his own, striking Balthazar as they both fell into an opening of the wormhole and landing in a desert.

"The hell are we?" Vail questioned.

Gazing around the desert, Vail turned around to see the Pyramids of Giza. However, they were not worn-out as they shined brightly with their white coating as the sun rose over them.

"We're in the past." Vail said to himself. "We're in Ancient Egypt."

Hearing the rush of dirt behind him, Vail turned as he saw Balthazar standing up from the fall. his eyes wandered around the desert during the clear day and he saw the glinting light of the pyramids. He turned toward Vail as he pointed at the pyramids.

"See! I told you! I have the power!"

"We can't stay here. We're going back."

"I'm going back. You will remain here!"

Another blast came from Balthazar's hands with Vail deflecting them once again. The energy from the Arch bolted from sky as Balthazar went to run for it. Vail followed him as he began to hear the sound of horses from behind. Turning to get a gaze, Vail saw the armies of the Pharaoh rushing toward them.

"Not what I was expecting this day to go."

Balthazar jumped into the bolting energy as Vail latched his hand onto Balthazar's cloak and the two went back into the wormhole just as the Egyptian army came near to them. Moving at great speed in the wormhole, the two continued their battle with Balthazar's energy blasts and Vail's fireballs. A second hole opened in the wormhole, causing them to fall into another set of sand. This time, Vail raised his head to find himself staring into the face of a lion. The lion lunged toward Vail, only for him to realize the lion was caged. The noise of a crowd shocked them as both Vail and Balthazar looked around.

"Where did you send us?" Balthazar said.

"You're the one with the traveling. But, I know where we are."

The crowds cheered and roared with excitement as Vail and Balthazar found themselves in the times of Ancient Rome, standing in the middle of the Roman Coliseum. The gates within the coliseum opened as armies of gladiators entered. Vail's hands conjured more flames as Balthazar's hands continued to glow. The gladiators looked at them, seeing their apparel and mocked as their hands gripped their swords and spears.

"You know what we have to do." Vail said.

"I'm not getting what you're saying."

"Until the beam comes down again, we'll have to work together to survive."

"They're nothing but brute beasts. What can a sword do against the might of magic."

The gladiators rushed into the fight against Vail and Balthazar. Vail deflected the swipes of their blades and retaliated with a flaming sword of his own. Formed from the flames on his hands. The embers shared from the clashing of the swords as Balthazar levitated himself above the battlefield, raining down energy blasts from his hands across the sands. The blasts knocked down the gladiators as the cages opened, releasing the lions. Vail looked as he saw the beasts charging toward them and a shockwave emitted from the sky, grabbing everyone's attention. The beam had returned and both Vail and Balthazar jumped in before the lions had them in their grasps. Moving around back through the wormhole, Vail could only wonder where they would end up next. Hoping they'll return to the Arch, the opening returned as the fell through, crashing on a road. Regaining themselves from the fall, Vail looked up, finding them both in a city lit by neon lighting. The streets were concrete just as the rain began to fall.

"What is this place?" Balthazar questioned. "The energy here is different."

Vail watched as the bystanders stared at them as if they were foreigners. Looking at the moving signs on the buildings describing the merging of humans and machines. One board presented a phrase Vail was not familiar with.

"For the Man-God?"

"We don't tolerate stranders in our city." A bystander yelled.

"Strander?" Vail said. "What the hell is that?"

The beam returned and they entered just as the bystanders began to move away in fear of someone else entering their city. All Vail could see before the beam took him and Balthazar was the silhouette of a hat and coat. Through the beam they went once more, now they fell onto a dead landscape. Nothing growing. Only the dirt remained. The sky above them shrouded in a dark red as if under a tent. The moon was red and the sun was unable to be found.

"I know where we are now." Vail said. "We're in the future."

"What future?" Balthazar questioned.

"The end of the world as we know it."

Around them, they could hear a battle taking place as lighting fell from the sky. Vail ran to see the battle and discovered it was covered with all the armies of the world and villains. Even some of the heroes were there in the fight. Many he did not recognize. There were others on the battlefield that was strange to Vail and Balthazar. They wielded swords of embedding light. A crack of thunder roamed over above them in the sky as the clouds began to open to the sound of a trumpet gathering everyone's attention. Some of the heroes had vanished while the armies and villains remained. Their eyes locked on the clouds and their weapons aimed.

"I know what this is." Vail said. "We're standing on the battlefields of Megiddo and He has returned."

Before Vail could see who was coming through the

clouds, the beam returned and gathered him and Balthazar as a bright flash of light poured from the clouds, covering the ground in a white shine in which the armies and villains were blinded by the sight. Through the wormhole once more and with a flash, Vail and Balthazar found themselves being tossed out of the Arch. Looking around as they found themselves back in St. Louis, Vail looked up, seeing Kamagratuto still in his place.

"Balthazar, shut this down!"

"I cannot. It is my purpose."

Vail shook his head with a low sigh, reaching into his jacket pocket taking out his book. Turning the page as Balthazar went to return to his twirling spell, Vail began to recite out of the book as the Arch's billowing energy slowly came to an end. Balthazar yelled as the energy evaporated from the Arch and his hands became still. There was no energy within him. Not even sparks emitted from his hands.

"What have you done to me?!"

"I only stopped you before you caused greater damage. Leave this city, Balthazar. Go find something productive outside the realm of magic."

"I will not be defeated this day!"

Balthazar went to strike Vail, yet was blocked by Kamagrauto who appeared in between the two men. Balthazar looked in terror at the lieutenant demon and teleported himself from the site. Vail was not amused.

"He does that every time."

"It appears it is over." Kamagrauto spoke.

"Yeah. Well, that ends the case for today."

The next day, Vail closed the case on the mysteries of
St. Louis as it was all the workings of Balthazar. Leaving the
city, Vail received a phone call from Gabriel Abraham.
Detailing some strange events taking place across the world.
The news of a darker presence had made itself known. This
is a case Vail knew for certain needed his expertise.

ABOUT THE AUTHOR

Ty'Ron W. C. Robinson II is the author of several works of fiction. Including the *Dark Titan Universe Saga, The Haunted City Saga, EverWar Universe, Symbolum Venatores, Frightened!, Instincts,* and others. More information pertaining to the books and stories can be found at darktitanpublishing.com

Follow The Universe of Realms:

Twitter: @DarkTitanBooks
Instagram: @darktitanbooks
TikTok: @thedarktitancompany